The Seekers

The Seekers

EILÍS DILLON

CHARLES SCRIBNER'S SONS | NEW YORK

Library of Congress Cataloging-in-Publication Data
Dillon, Eilís, 1920-   The seekers.
Summary: Sixteen-year-old Edward sails with friends
from England to the New World in 1632 and joins the
colony founded by the Pilgrims at Plymouth, discovering
the perils and hardships of colonial life.
[1. Pilgrims (New Plymouth Colony)—Fiction.
2. Massachusetts—Social life and customs—
Colonial period, ca. 1600-1775—Fiction] I. Title.
PZ7.D5792Sg   1986   [Fic]   85-43347
ISBN 0-684-18595-4

1 3 5 7 9 11 13 15 17 19   F/C   20 18 16 14 12 10 8 6 4 2

Printed in the United States of America

FOR TINA
Who first took me to New Plymouth

One

THIS STORY BEGINS IN 1632, when I was sixteen years old and living with my parents and my grandmother in a quiet village in Yorkshire, in the north of England. I was the youngest of the family and the only one still living at home. My two older sisters were already married and had children of their own. My three brothers had gone off to trades and were prospering, one a stonemason, one a blacksmith, and the one next to me, John, was — of all things — a ship carpenter. When I went to stay a few days with them now and then, I was naturally put to work and so acquired a little of each of these skills.

To understand why you should be surprised at John's having that particular trade you must first know that Beacon, our village, is a good forty miles from the sea, on a high, windy hillside. How John got the idea of building ships I know not, but he was said to be very good at it.

Quiet it was indeed in Beacon. The parson's sermon on Sunday was often the most exciting event of the week.

Everyone knew everyone else's business, which had its good as well as its bad side. If someone was sick or in trouble, the neighbors might smirk to themselves as if to say they knew why misfortune fell there and at that time, but they would always go and lend a hand where they could. One or two families seemed almost to attract trouble.

My father was Peter Deane, known to everyone as a careful, sensible man. He made a living from a flock of sheep that he took from one common to another, as necessary. He sold the wool in summer after the shearing, to merchants in Bawtry or even in Epworth, but he always kept enough for us at home. He rented some land to grow corn and vegetables for our needs and some to sell. He kept a few cows and goats that gave us plenty of milk. Sometimes he worked for our landlord, but he always managed to keep enough time for his own affairs.

My mother was named Sarah Bell. She had come north from Suffolk and was never done with grumbling at the cold of Yorkshire. She would not believe there was any place colder in the whole world, where the chickens died and the cabbages withered in the winter blasts. In all the years since she had married my father, she had never once gone home to visit her own people. Her sisters wrote and sent messages inviting her, but there was always a good reason why she couldn't go. First there were the children who couldn't be left when they were small. Then there was the cooking and cleaning and weaving and sewing and knitting for the whole family. At last, when no one was left but myself, there was my grandmother.

Granny Meg was my father's mother, Margaret Deane. She had lived with us since my grandfather died, before I was born. Now that she was old, my mother said that she must not be left alone to look after the house and that if she went south Granny Meg would not last a week. The truth was that the time for going south was long gone, and my mother had never really wanted to travel at all. If you had asked me when I was sixteen, I would have agreed that there was no sense to leaving home unless you were driven to it.

I went to school with Deacon Graves long enough to learn to read and write, and then my father needed my help with the sheep. I never regretted it. My greatest pleasure when I was small was to spend long summer days on the high, rolling hills, watching the great clouds go sailing by, fishing in the bright streams, making a shelter here and there at night as necessary. Then we would build a big fire to keep off the dark and huddle together around it. We were always two or three families for company and safety.

I and the other boys had plenty of time for amusement during the long days, since sheep don't move about very much. We knew every stream that fed the river Idle, and if I were blindfolded, I could still tell on which part of the bank I was standing by the sound of the water trickling over the bed of the stream.

My particular friend was Andrew Hogdon. He was three years older than I, but it made no difference. He became my friend when I taught him to read. Though his father was quite well off, he never troubled himself much with education. He owned a tavern, and he reckoned that one needed only a little ciphering for that, as well as a good knowledge of human nature. He died in the big plague and left his money to Andrew, but he also left him a great distaste for crowded rooms and shouting, drinking men. This was why he wanted to learn to read, he said, so that he could travel the world.

"Why should you leave Yorkshire?" I asked. "There can be no better place anywhere."

He gave me a strange look, but he made no reply. Whenever this happened I was hurt by it, knowing that it meant he felt so much older and wiser than I was.

He walked away from me, as if he were thinking over his future and what he would do with it. Without a trade, without the tavern, which he said he hated, with no patience for the daily work of farming, what was left for him? I could never imagine that he would be content with minding sheep, though one could travel all over England, at least, with them.

We had that conversation on a beautiful morning in early May. There was a little bite in the air, as if there had been a light frost during the night. We had come up early to see how the lambs were doing. My cousin Zachary had been in charge of them for the past month, and he had been boasting that this was the best year we had had for a long time.

I said, "I'd like to crossbreed the Blackfaces with Border Leicesters. We'd get stronger animals and better wool, if it worked."

"You're a real Yorkshire man," Andrew said. "What does your father say about it?"

"He's willing to try. It won't cost anything."

I began to describe what I had planned, the time of year, what the lambs would look like, until I saw that he had no interest in what I was saying. He turned suddenly and said, "There are countries in the world with huge forests, and lakes like oceans, and rivers so broad that you can barely see to the far bank, lions, bears — I can't live with sheep, when I know all those wonders are there to be seen. Someday I'll sail all the seas of the world."

"I don't care if I never see a bear. I like to be able to see across the river. I hope I'll never sail the ocean until the day I die," I said just as hotly.

"I would go tomorrow, if I knew how it was done," he said with a note of infinite longing in his voice.

Apart from any ideas about sheep-breeding, I had a very good reason for wanting to stay in Beacon. Our nearest neighbor, Moses Moore, was a widower with one daughter, Rebecca. She was a year younger than I, and ever since I was five years old I had been in love with her.

You may think five too young an age for feelings like mine, but I can assure you that this is true. The Deanes are all tall and dark and bushy-haired, the men with great black beards that have to be trimmed as often as a hedge. Rebecca was fair-skinned and golden-haired, like the angels in the church windows. That was what started it, perhaps, but she was also the best companion for every one of my games, from pretending we were king and queen to fishing in the Idle. And she was clever, too. When I was teaching Andrew, she always sat on the grass near us and repeated everything I said, and she learned as quickly as he did.

I waited until I was twelve to ask her to marry me and she said, "Of course. You couldn't marry anyone else."

So it was settled, and though we didn't talk about it much, everything I did from then onward was working toward that goal.

I was very fond of Granny Meg, and it was a great pleasure to me that Rebecca was, too. Granny Meg used to say that with all the children grown up she had never enough to do, and it was her delight to teach Rebecca all the skills she had. While my mother was out in the fields with my father, they would sit together by the hour while Granny Meg watched Rebecca card wool until she had a long, thin piece that you could nearly blow away with your breath. Then she would take out the big spinning wheel, and they would work together at making the thread, singing strange old songs that matched the song of the wheel. On other days they would bake cakes, and then we would sit around the table for hours eating them, until Granny Meg would suddenly say, "Another baking day gone to waste! Where have all the cakes gone?"

And she would pretend to chase us around the house with the broom until she collapsed, laughing, into the big rocking chair, her special chair, by the fire.

Rebecca's Aunt Abigail, her father's sister, lived with the Moores. She was a widow, and you would think she would know enough about keeping house to take over her brother's affairs. They were very simple, but it seemed that Aunt Abigail had forgotten everything she had ever known about housekeeping. When she set a clutch of eggs, she always forgot the date or put in the wrong eggs or did some other foolish thing that no one else would ever think of. When there were chickens, the cat ate them; then the dog killed the cat. As if that were not enough, the mice ate the meal, the water barrel leaked, weevils got into the flour — something always happened to bring Aunt Abigail scurrying over to our house for comfort from Granny Meg. Besides, she never seemed to sweep the floor or dust the dresser or do any of the things the other women did to make the house look neat and comfortable. As for baking bread or roasting meat, she seemed not to know where to begin. If it hadn't been for Rebecca, Granny Meg said, all three of them would have starved to death.

One September evening, I came home from the fields where I had been helping my father with the threshing, to find Rebecca sitting silently by the fire. I was so glad

7

to see her that I called out at once, "We've finished! Dancing tonight, Becky!"

She looked up at me sorrowfully, then down again into the ashes.

"What's happened?" I said. "Can't you come?"

I could imagine no greater misfortune than that she would not be with me at the dance. Parson made no objection to it at harvest time, so long as everyone went home immediately afterward and there was no loitering by the hedges. He usually came along to see that those rules were obeyed.

"Indeed I can come," Rebecca said, "but this will be the last harvest."

"What do you mean?"

"Father . . . Father. . . ." She burst out crying, and I could get no more out of her until Granny Meg came in from the yard with the empty basin from which she had been feeding the little pigs.

"What now? What's going on?" she said.

"I don't know," I said, wishing I could cry myself.

"Come now, Becky," Granny Meg said. "It can't be so bad. What has happened?"

"The worst," she said fiercely, suddenly no longer crying. "Father — he was always talking about the New World, how he wanted to go there long ago and they would never let him, and now he's determined to take ship and sail off and take me with him."

"Who wouldn't let him? He could do what he liked, surely," I said, doubting her story at once.

8

"It's true," Granny Meg said. "He wanted to go when the first party went, but they said he was too profane and they left him behind. I thought he had put it out of his head."

"He went to the tavern last night," Rebecca said, "and there was a sailor who said the New World is a paradise, and everyone lives in a fine house and wears furs and eats meat and fish every day and has gold in store as well. Father can talk of nothing else. All day he has been telling us of the new life we're going to have — "

"Aunt Abigail, too?" Granny Meg chuckled. "I'd like to be there to see her tackle some of the things the women have to do in New England."

"She hasn't decided to come," Rebecca said, "and Father says it's up to her to make up her mind. But I have no choice, he said, because he's my father and can tell me what to do."

"I'll have a thing or two to say to him," Granny Meg said. "Silly old fool, at his age. Not that you're entitled to think of him like that, miss. He's your father, and you must do as he says, whatever it is, even foolishness."

"Why should she?" I said. "That's just more foolishness."

"But it's the way of the world," Granny Meg said. "There's no getting away from it."

We went to the dance, and Rebecca forgot some of her fears while we whirled and frisked and ate apples and cakes, as we always did at harvest time. There were games of throwing sheaves, and Andrew was the champion.

Everyone was amazed, since he owned no land and always said he didn't care a fig for farming. It was the best time of the year, when no one believed in hunger or cold or poverty any longer, just in fun and enjoyment and dancing.

The Saints — those who had gone to the New World and who said Moses Moore was too profane to be of their company — they would never agree to the harvest dancing. They said it was the devil's work and anyone who joined in was damned in the next world forever. I couldn't believe in that. It was one of the reasons why I couldn't believe either that they were living such a high life now, with furs and gold. If they had those things, surely they would think them sinful.

I didn't wonder that they had refused to take Moses with them. He was fond of a drop, when he could get it, and he would tell stories that were not fit for good company. He was not their kind at all — he didn't even go to church on Sunday if he thought he had something better to do with his time. Other than that, he was a peaceful man, though not much good to work. I couldn't imagine my Rebecca in the forbidding company of the Saints.

On the way home I said, "You must tell your father you can't go with him."

"How can I?" she said. "He can't go alone."

"Aunt Abigail can go."

"She says she's not sure she wants to go, and besides, she's too silly. I know I shouldn't say it about my own father, but I think he's too silly as well. God knows I don't want to leave England, nor to leave you, but what can I do? Granny Meg agrees with me. She has a small opinion of both of them. She says they'll die if I'm not there to take care of them."

I said harshly, "And what about you? Will they notice if you die?"

"I can't help it," she said. "I couldn't leave my own father. And perhaps what they say is true, that we'll get rich and have all those furs to wear and meat every day of the week — "

"You don't believe that, do you?" I said.

"No. But I'm sorry for my father. He doesn't know he's too old for all that now. How can I tell him?"

I had to agree that it was impossible. My mother and father joined in the discussion, and all agreed that Rebecca must go with her father to take care of him.

"It can't be that bad," my mother said. "People have been there and come back alive. Some say it's all right if you can work hard and if you don't complain."

That was cold comfort, but it was the best they could do. Rebecca said very little after that first conversation, but I knew she was afraid. Throughout that winter I went very often to the Moores and sat looking at her, thinking I might never see her again. Her father seemed to me rather apologetic, as if he were trying to explain what was in his mind. He knew we were fond of each other, but he had an idea that his rights came before mine.

"I've never had a chance," he said one evening. "Your chances will come. When the Saints went to the New World, I thought my time had come, but I found it had not. Wait your time, my boy. Give me mine, now that I have it in sight."

What could I say? It was a cry from the heart. "Do what you must," I mumbled.

In the spring he began to sell up the few bits and pieces he owned. The neighbors bought them out of charity only, for they were hardly worth the haul home — broken chairs and tables, mattresses so thin a dog wouldn't sleep on them, a dresser that had more worm than wood in it, an ancient cow that hadn't given milk for three years, sheep that were bald as an egg, goats that were so hungry they would eat the fencing around their field — even the chickens were spun out with age. Moses strutted around as if he were doing a kindness to the community by disposing of this rubbish, and as if he were about to embark on a voyage that was certain to end in a river of gold. Neighbors laughed behind their hands, but they were sorry for him, too.

The day they left was a sad one for me. I could scarcely believe the moment had come. I had thought until now that some good sense would intervene and stop this madness. From the moment I knew Aunt Abigail was going, too, I despaired. She added to her brother's excitement, rather than restraining him. After her first doubts, she had become enthusiastic about the plan and had taken to boasting to the other women about the good times that were in store for her. No one in England had a real chance to show what they could do, she said. New England was the land of opportunity, where everyone started equal and you got rich through your own efforts.

One or two looked doubtful, almost as if they believed her, and she climbed into the cart that was to take them to Plymouth well pleased with herself.

I had nothing to say. Though I had my plans, I couldn't open my mouth about them. I had to endure the sight of Rebecca in floods of tears and keep dead silence. Without a word, I walked home with Granny Meg as if I had resigned myself to the parting.

Two

Six o'clock on a morning in March is a cold time for saying good-bye to someone you love as I did Rebecca. Long after the cart had gone, I could see her in my mind's eye huddled in a shawl, leaning against Aunt Abigail, trying not to show her grief and despair at leaving me. We were too young to have any rights. We belonged to our parents.

I went quickly to Andrew Hogdon's house. He was my only possible help now. He was up and about, though he hadn't come to see the Moores off. I had missed him there — indeed I was angry that he hadn't bestirred himself to come, since he knew how much I cared for Rebecca, and he had always been such a friend of hers, too.

"Why didn't you come to see the cart go?" I asked at once, hardly knowing what I was saying. "You'll never see her again."

"Oh, yes, I will," he said, too calmly I thought.

I had found him in the stable rubbing down his horse,

a tall bay gelding of eighteen hands. They suited each other, that thin, gangling pair.

"What do you mean?" I said. "She's gone, I tell you — gone for good. She can never, never come back. I have such a pain on me that I'd like to die this moment, if I could."

"You will go after her. When you do, so will I."

"How can I go after her? How do you know I want to?"

"I don't take you for a fool. Would you let her go like that, with those silly relatives of hers, and never do anything about her? Perhaps you're too fond of your sheep to leave them."

"What's the use of talking about what I would like to do?" I said. "I have no money. I can't go. I know nothing about ships. No one would take me on one, unless I could pay my passage."

"So you have thought of that way."

He led the horse out of the stable into the yard. Two mongrel dogs gamboled around the horse's hooves, hoping they were all going to set out for a ride. But Andrew hitched the horse to the fence and made for the house, saying to me, "Come inside and we'll talk about it."

I did as I was told, too numb with pain to think about what was in his mind. Since his father's death Andrew lived alone, with only cats and dogs for company. Every time I went to his house, there seemed to be more and more of these beasts, roosting on the chair backs, growling from the hearthstone, or pacing up and down outside like little watchmen. And the house itself was as wild as the animals that lived in it. One almost expected to see bushes growing up through the kitchen floor and grass sprouting from the walls. His pallet in the corner was like a dog's bed. Granny Meg always worried about him since he was left alone.

"He'll turn into a dog himself some day." she said. "If his poor mother could only see him!"

But his mother had died when he was ten years old, and neither he nor his father had bothered with civilized living since then.

He threw himself into a chair beside the dead hearth and said, "You don't have to be a sailor to cross the sea."

"A sailor or a rich man. My father has nothing, even if he wanted to give me the passage money. The harvest money is long gone. It went on the rent. Now we wait until the lambs are grown, then until the shearing, then until the harvest again."

I was not bitter about it. This was our way of life. It was like the turning of the seasons. We didn't need much money. We had little use for it. Now for the first time in my life I wished I had a purse full of golden guineas. I might as well have longed for the moon.

"If I tell you about my plan, I wonder if you will have the courage for it." Andrew said.

"Courage?" My hands began to sweat, though I had only a faint inkling of what was in his mind. Talk, fan-

tastic ideas, seemed suddenly about to become realities.
I was not at all sure that I had the courage he expected
of me, but I said boldly, "If courage is all I need, I have
plenty of it. But what can I do?"

"Come with me to Plymouth. We'll follow them all
the way to the sea."

"Leave Beacon? Follow them?" I said stupidly.

One of the wild plans that had been whirling around
in my head was that I would walk after them every step
of the way, hiding by night and keeping them in sight.
You would need to know Beacon village to understand
what a crazy plan that was. Andrew was laughing at me.

"Why not?" he said. "I have enough money for both
of us. Look!"

He lifted a loose stone out of the chimney breast,
using the fingers and thumbs of both hands to get it
free. I could never have guessed that it could be so easily
moved. He laid the stone carefully on the hearth and
reached inside the hollow that it had left exposed. In a
moment he had pulled out a soft leather bag that jingled
in his hands. He dropped it on the kitchen table with a
thump, then tipped it sideways and spilled a river of
gold onto the dirty boards.

"Look at it," he said, "the sweat of the people of
Beacon, the bread of the poor wives and children, the
hopes of widows and orphans."

"What do you mean?"

"The profits from our tavern — I detest these gold

pieces. Often I've wanted to take them down to the Idle bridge and throw them into the river, get rid of them. It's dirty money, though it shines like the sun."

"I didn't know you felt so bad about it."

He had told me that he could never carry on his father's trade, but I had thought it harmless enough. When my own father went now and then for a quiet drink with his friends, I had never believed the tavern was the vestibule to Hell, as Parson said it was. My mother's ale was usually good enough for us, but now and then my father liked to make his own company and perhaps taste strong waters for a change. Some of the men never knew when to go home, but I always regarded these as the exceptions.

Andrew was watching me.

"You're shocked," he said. "You haven't lived close to it as I have." He picked up a few of the coins and let them trickle through his fingers. "I want to get as far as possible from the source of this wealth. I've always told you — the wilderness — the trees — the huge rivers — the animals — nothing will keep me away from them now. We'll go together."

He pushed the gold back into the bag and twisted the neck, replaced it in the hole by the fireplace, and fitted the stone back into place. How simple it was for him! For me it would be an upheaval, the like of which I had never really contemplated.

"My father and mother," I said. "What can I say to them?"

"It's true, it will be hard for them. But they must know you will leave home some day and make your own life."

"No, that was never to be. I was to carry on as my father did, with the sheep and the land."

He was silent for a while, and I could see that he thought this a very strange idea. Then he said, "I'll not press you. I just know that if my girl were on her way across the wide ocean, I would be with her no matter what the cost. You must think about it for a day or two. This is Tuesday. If we want to catch up with them, we should be on our way by Friday at the latest. I'm going to ride after them come what may. I'm in the way of getting another horse. If you want to come with me, you're welcome."

That was all. I went home, full of fears and suspicions and wild longings. If Andrew were to appear, riding his tall horse, and help Rebecca on her journey as he was planning to do, who could tell but that she might forget me and put him in my place? I could almost have hated him for the very idea. But I knew he was my friend, and my only hope, too. Besides, I had always known that I would follow her. I had had no idea how it could be done. Now that it was all clear, there was nothing more to wait for.

I didn't wait until Friday to tell Andrew about my decision. By the very next morning I knew what I had to do. The hardest part was concealing my plan from my parents. I don't know why I thought it would be easier for them if I didn't confront them with my decision but let them find it out after I was gone. Now I think I was wrong. It would have spared them great pain to have known what was in my mind, and I don't believe now that they would have stopped me.

What I did was for the best as I saw it. I wrote them a careful letter, which I knew they would have to take to Parson to read since neither of them could read writing other than the printed Bible.

The words are fixed in my memory:

"Dear Father and Mother, my Rebecca has gone to New England. If I want to take care of her safety, I must follow her. We will come home as soon as we can. Please do not worry about us, only pray that we may meet again some day on this earth."

I left my letter on the kitchen table, placing a mug on top in case the cats should tear it. Then I set out for Andrew's house. It was early morning, just after dawn. Granny Meg was not yet out of bed, but my parents were already in the fields and would soon begin to wonder why I was not following them. I thought of telling Granny Meg what I was going to do, but even with her I felt that I had to be silent. Andrew was already up and about. I almost ran into his house, crying out, "Here I am. When are we going?"

Andrew said calmly, "I was expecting you. I knew you wouldn't wait beyond this morning." He was busy herding the animals out of the house. He said, "The horses are ready."

"One for me, too?" I said.

"Yes. I bought Jacob Burns' horse for three guineas. It's a good strong pony — 'twill carry you all the way for certain."

"The dogs and cats? What about them?"

"Someone always takes care of them," he said. Then, seeing my anxiety, he laughed. "What an old fusspot you are. Goody Harfield will see to them. Do you think I would forget them?"

I should have known he would have found someone. I asked, "Will she keep them until you come home?"

Andrew looked at me with an expression I couldn't understand, then said, "Yes, she will keep them."

He had a small cloth bag ready, which he slung outside the door. I had one of the same size, containing a change of clothes and three books. Now that we were about to go, I was excited and pleased at the adventure and cared nothing for what we would take with us. Andrew looked at my bundle and said, "Good. Not too much, not too little."

He locked the door carefully and put the heavy iron key in his pocket. He stood for a moment gazing around the yard, as if he had forgotten something, then said, "Time to go."

He picked up his bag and leaped onto his horse. The one he had bought for me was slightly smaller, and quieter, too, for which I was glad. I hung my bag by its strings from the saddle and followed him out of the yard.

We left the village quietly, the horses moving on the grass as if they knew we had no wish to attract attention. In a few minutes we had left the houses behind and were riding down the Great North Road. That was a fine name for the track that connected us with London and the south of England, where the ships were. It was no more than a wide, worn path, with trees on either side almost too close for comfort. It was true that an order had come down from London to cut these back to a distance of two hundred feet on either side so that the highwaymen couldn't hide so easily, but it takes more than that to put a highwayman off his living. We traveled safely enough, because we looked too poor to be interesting, but it was not pleasant to know that if we had been rich we would never have seen the Abbey and Hall of Westminster.

I think it was the greatest moment in all my life when we rode over the top of a hill and looked down at the city of London. I pulled in my horse, who was impatient at the delay. We had not done as the rich do, changing horses at the inns every twenty miles or so. Ours had to keep to the road at our speed, with no complaints. It was not a hard journey, because we made sure not to catch up with the cart that was carrying the Moores. This was much slower than a couple of healthy horses, and there were long stops on the road when we had to rest in spite of ourselves.

Andrew pulled in beside me and said, "There it is, my first sight of it. I hope it may be my last."

I was shocked. "Why? Why? That's where the king lives, the father of all of us."

"Father? Well, perhaps."

I had no patience with him. I would have given anything to see the king pass by on his way to the hunt, surrounded by his lords and ladies, the whole party dressed in gold and red velvet and riding splendid horses. I said nothing to Andrew about this, lest he might think me a fool. We sat for a while to gaze at the winding river Thames, with the spring sun glinting on it and the shadows of the great bridges making oval loops in the still water. At last he said, "It is a fine city indeed, but before I die I hope to see finer sights."

We rode into the city then and found lodgings in a mean street near the river. It seemed to me that the people here were much noisier than they were in the North. We went down to the water's edge to look at the traffic there. Dozens of boats were plying in every direction, watermen yelling at each other in a language that I could scarcely understand, though I knew it was English, ships standing out to sea with full sail, impatient passengers waiting for transport as if their lives depended on it — one felt weak, just to watch them.

But Andrew was delighted with the river. When I

turned to say that all sensible people should stay at home, I saw that his eyes were shining with excitement when they rested on the ships.

"We'll find one like the best of them," he said, "fit to sail the seven seas. We'll sail to the farthest shores of the whole world."

"Just to New England," I said. "That will be enough for me."

We spent only one night in London. It was no place for horses. They put them into the stables at the inn, but during the night men came to see if any were worth stealing. We found this out in the morning, when the innkeeper told us that he had caught the robbers in the act and that they were now in Newgate jail.

Though I had been so pleased at my first sight of London, I agreed at once when Andrew said that we should get on our way as soon as possible. Never in my life had I seen so many beggars, nor so many miserable, unfortunate people. In Yorkshire we were poor, indeed, but it had not led us to depravity as it had done with these people.

We had not spoken to the Moores since our departure, but we had kept close enough to see their cart often. This was Andrew's decree, though I would have been glad to have traveled with them after the first few days, so as to let Rebecca know that I was close to her and keeping watch for her. Andrew said that this would not do, that Moses would raise a shout that I was trying to abduct his daughter, and that I would end up in prison. To risk that would be foolish, and I heeded his advice. Indeed, by now I had come to see that Andrew was wise and knowledgable and that I would do well to obey him in everything.

If London pleased and overawed me, Plymouth amazed me. The town was placed at the inner end of a long sound, well sheltered from the wind. There were three small harbors, each containing a variety of boats of all sizes, from fishing smacks to ships of a hundred tons and more, fit to take one to the ends of the earth. Watermen plied back and forth to the bigger ships, just as they did in London, carrying cargo and passengers from the sandy shore. My brother John had shown me the wonders of Hull, where he built wherries for crossing the mud flats and for fishing, but never in this life had I thought to see such tall, stately ships as were in the roadsteads of Plymouth.

Andrew was in his element. He picked a lodging close to the harbor named Cattewater, in a tumbledown house that seemed to have been repaired many times with oddments of driftwood from the shore. The innkeeper looked as if he had been washed up on the shore himself, some dark night after a storm.

"A bed?" he growled at us. "Who cares about a bed? A roof is what you want and it's what you'll get. A bed is a riddle at the best of times." He looked at our horses. "Where did you get them beasts?"

"Bred them from good Yorkshire mares," said Andrew. It was true, for the horse he had bought for me was one he had sold to Burns as a foal. "I'll make a bargain with you."

"Bargain?" said the innkeeper. "No one makes a bargain with me."

"This is a bargain you won't refuse," Andrew said, as bold as brass. "You can give us lodging for as long as we stay in Plymouth. Then, when we take ship, we'll leave you the horses for your own use. When my friend here comes back, you'll give him back one horse and room for as many nights as he wants to stay."

The innkeeper gave a shout of laughter.

"And what about yourself? Won't you be wanting your horse back, too?"

"Never again, if I have my way," Andrew said.

It was the first time he had said it plainly, and though I had guessed what was in his mind, still I was shocked through and through. The innkeeper accepted the bargain and made me write it out on a piece of dirty paper, which he buried inside his greasy shirt.

As we walked down to the port I said, "I'm sorry to hear from you that you will never come back."

"Never is a long time," he said. "I think there are a great many things to see. Who knows but I'll come back some day?"

I had to be content with that. At least he was not going to leave me yet. I asked, "Why did you pick that hole, and that scoundrel?"

"Because I think Moses Moore will not dare to come there. His sister won't allow it."

"Aunt Abigail? She doesn't give the orders in that house."

"Before we left, I thought she was beginning to lift her head higher than I ever saw her do before. Tomorrow I'll find out where they are staying and if they have found a ship to take them."

Three

So WE SPENT A NIGHT with bedbugs and fleas and snoring customers of the inn, all lying side by side in a huge room that seemed devoid of air. I thought of the high, bare hills of Yorkshire, the nights around the fire while the sheep wandered close by and we lay together under the stars. We slept with our bags as pillows, for safety. Riding is a tiring business, and perhaps fatigue came to our aid. I hoped Rebecca was better lodged than I was, and I wished that she would some day come to know what I was suffering for her sake.

You may be sure we didn't sleep late. Andrew moved before I did, unable to stand the stench a moment longer, and I followed him quickly outside. We found a sort of latrine at the back of the inn and were glad to be the first there. Andrew said, "No ship could be worse than what we have endured this night. I'll go at once and see what I can find. Better for you to stay here, out of sight. One person attracts less attention than two."

"Where will you go?"

"To the waterfront." Seeing my distraught expression he said, "Come with me, then, but if you see Moses Moore, be sure that he doesn't see you."

"He's the cause of all my trouble."

"Fools always cause more trouble than wise men," Andrew said.

The port was humming with life and energy. As we arrived, a three-masted ship in full sail was setting out to sea. Shallops darted in and out among the ships lying at anchor, their single sails turning with every wind, the men like riders, changing position with every move of their craft. Above all it looked so clean, by comparison with the filthy land, where the mud and offal covered the street and the drains ran with household waste, which stank in the nostrils.

When we were almost at the Cattewater, there came Moses Moore. He was swaggering — that is the only word for his gait. In Beacon he had always seemed to be apologizing for his existence, rightly as most of his neighbors thought. He would drag one foot after him, as if he hoped you would pity him enough to let him use the road. Now his chest was thrown out, his hands in his pockets, and his head moving arrogantly from side to side as he surveyed the busy scene.

Andrew said, "Out of the way, while you can."

I did as I was told, though I couldn't have borne it if Rebecca had been with him. I slipped into an alley and watched him, half glad to see him so pleased with himself. Andrew made sure not to draw attention to himself, naturally, and Moses passed him by without recognizing him. With so many people about, he would never have expected to see someone from home.

Just before he would have passed the end of my alley, he turned off to the right as if he knew exactly where he was going.

Andrew came back and said, "That must be the direction of his lodging. I think he must have found a ship to carry him. He looked like my cat Pouncer when she gets a rat."

"Which ship?"

"That will take time to discover. Why don't you follow him at a distance? If you keep out of sight, you may be able to find out where they are all staying."

I needed no second bidding. Moses was marching along fast, but I could still see him. It was easy to keep close enough in the crowded street. Presently he stopped at a decent-looking inn, much better than ours. There was a bench outside the door, where customers could sit and drink their beer, and while I watched, a woman came out and rubbed it clean with a cloth. No one at our inn had rubbed anything with a cloth for a long time. I was pleased that Rebecca was being given a good lodging, at least.

I was at a loss what to do next. Fate decided it. I was planning to stand there, staring at the house that contained my love, all night long if necessary, when suddenly the door opened and out she came.

What was I to do? Caution told me to wait a little, until she walked away from the inn and then, after a short pause to make up her mind, turned into a side street. Like Andrew's Pouncer stalking a bird, I followed her. She walked slowly, as if she had no special errand to do. I was in luck that Aunt Abigail was foolish enough to let her out alone. Already I had sensed that a girl couldn't run free here, as she could do in perfect safety at home.

After a while the street became a track that ran off into the fields. Where the houses ended, a flock of geese was grazing on a patch of grass. A little girl, armed with a long stick, was minding them. Rebecca stopped to watch them, then called out something to the little girl. There was no one else near. It seemed that all the life of the town was down at the port. One or two houses opened onto the green. This was my chance. I called out, "Rebecca!"

She whirled around and stared wildly at me as if she didn't know me. Then she came running into my arms, laughing and shivering and barely able to speak. With her head on my chest she said shakily, "I thought I would never see you again. I thought Aunt Abigail was teasing me. She said you were following us."

"Aunt Abigail! She knew nothing about it."

"She said she saw you, and Andrew, too, on horses, a long way back."

"Did she tell anyone else?"

"No. She said she would tell no one."

"We were never very far away. Rebecca, I must come with you. I couldn't let you face out there alone."

The first question she asked was, "Do your parents know?"

"I left them a letter."

"You did this for me?"

"I would do anything in the world for you."

With our arms around each other's waists, we strolled onto the green. It was so picked over by the geese that the grass was worn thin. Besides, the spring rain had made it into a sea of mud. We soon left it again and walked along the track, out into the country. I think we cared about nothing then except that we were together, though heaven knows we should have been anxious about the dangers in front of us.

I couldn't decide whether or not she should tell her father that I was going to sail with them. If I hadn't seen him in his new style, I might have thought it better to come out into the open. But the Moses I had seen was someone I had never known in my life. There was no telling what he would do. Aunt Abigail must have changed, too, if she was able to keep herself from telling a secret.

Rebecca agreed that Andrew and I should try to keep out of sight as long as possible. This meant that we could not meet again. We walked back to the town silently, clinging to each other until the last moment before she had to turn off to go to her lodging.

I went down to the harbor to look for Andrew. There was a stiff March breeze, and I hugged my sheepskin jacket around me to keep warm. A short pier, or mole, ran out into the water, providing shelter for a few small boats and forming a breakwater to keep the harbor calm. Andrew was leaning against the low wall of the breakwater, talking to an older man who was dressed in a tarred coat that almost reached to his heels. When I came up, Andrew said, "Here is my friend now. Just in time, Edward. Captain Mullins is taking us on *The Swallow* tonight."

"All paid up and ready to go," the captain said. "A good, clean ship. Never carried a dirty cargo in her life. There she is." He pointed to a large ship, or so she seemed to me then, lying a quarter of a mile off the shore. She had two masts and she stood high in the water, with deckhouses fore and aft. "New England is a good country for the young, but I wouldn't like to try it at my age. I was telling your friend here that an old fellow asked me for a passage this morning — taking his sister and his young daughter with him. Madness, I said, but he wouldn't listen to me. Comes from your part of the world, too — funny way of talking they have in those parts, meaning no offense."

I kept a straight face, from politeness. The captain's accent made his English seem almost like a foreign language to me, each vowel stretched out until it sounded like two. It was even worse than what I had heard in London. And some of the words he used I had never heard before. I could only guess at their meaning. A good many of the sailors spoke in that same way, being mostly Devon and Cornish men, as we found out later.

The captain told Andrew what we would need for the voyage, and said in a low voice, "Take that gold out of your pocket one piece at a time. Don't let anyone see how much you have, or you'll never set foot on *The Swallow*."

This warning made us nervous. We went to a shop nearby, very dark inside, and Andrew gave an order for food and two pallets to lie on, as well as some blankets and rugs. The shopkeeper gave us good advice about what to buy — dried fish, cheese, and hard ship's biscuit, aniseed water to make hot drinks, and a keg of butter. Beer would be supplied on the ship. We could take fresh meat, too, and the sailors would salt it for us during the voyage. He sold us a small brazier, and a pot to cook in, and a bag of charcoal. Then he said, "How about some lemons and sugar? I have a nice lot, come in two days ago from Spain. Lemons keep off the scurvy, as every gentleman knows."

"We're not gentlemen," Andrew said, "but we'll have the lemons all the same."

The shopkeeper said we should also take olive oil, which had come from Spain with the lemons, and cotton yarn for lampwicks, and a roll of paper and some linseed oil to make windows, in case we wanted to build a house in the new country. He asked about our clothes and sold us each two pairs of trousers and several shirts. Andrew picked out two long-barreled guns, with powder and shot, and hooks and lines for fishing. All of these things were to be packed in canvas sacks and sent down to the harbor, labeled in Andrew's name.

As we had some hours to go before the shallop would take us to the ship, we went to an eating house in the neighborhood of our own inn. We had a beef pasty, the last for a long time, and fair, white bread of a kind I had never tasted before. When we said we were to sail that day, the landlord gave us some of a sack posset that he had prepared for a special customer. The landlord was named Bob Priestley, and the thought of his kindness comforted me many a time in the weeks that followed.

As we sat sipping the posset, I told Andrew about my conversation with Rebecca and how Aunt Abigail had said she saw us.

He chuckled, saying, "I told you there was a change in her. It's good for you to have an ally in this adventure."

"You're sure it was Goodman Moore who took passage on *The Swallow?*"

"We won't board her until we see them go on first," he said.

What would happen then was something I couldn't afford to consider. I only knew that Captain Mullins would be very unlikely to turn back and put me ashore on orders from Moses Moore.

We had not long to wait. We had taken up a position a short distance from the start of the quay, where some barrels lay ready for loading. We had not been there more than ten minutes when a little procession appeared, Moses marching out in front, Aunt Abigail almost running to keep up with him, her neck stretched like a questing hen, and last of all my lovely Rebecca.

She was the only one who was looking around her. The other two had their eyes fixed on the quay and the ship that was to take us all away.

Rebecca saw us and gave a small wave of her free hand. She was carrying a handbag, like Aunt Abigail. The rest of their possessions followed them on a barrow, pushed by a man from the inn. A sailor was waiting for them on the shore to direct them to a shallop that was filling up with other passengers. We watched while they climbed on board and settled themselves with their baggage around their feet. Then the shallop pushed off and set out for *The Swallow*.

Now I was in a state of terror lest we might see the shallop hauled on board and *The Swallow* hoist sail without waiting for us. Nothing of the sort happened, and I was glad I had not mentioned my fears to poor, patient Andrew. We soon saw the shallop unload and turn about, and when she beached by the quay we were ready waiting and were the first to board her.

It seemed to take an age for the second trip to begin. I had no patience with the other passengers. They were all as nervous as I was. Most of them were silent and white-faced, but one family made enough noise for a regiment. It consisted of a man named Price and two grown sons who kept pestering the sailors in charge of the shallop because they said some of their baggage had been left on the shore. They counted and counted again and at last had to admit that every one of their packages was there. Then they threw suspicious looks at the rest of us, as if they thought we were out to steal from them. At last Andrew addressed the father quietly, saying, "Sir, if I were you, I wouldn't begin such a long voyage by making a disturbance. We must live together for weeks, maybe months. Unless everyone gives way a little, there will be no peace for anyone."

The man glared at him, clenching his fists, then dropped his eyes and mumbled, "It's all right, now. We have no reason to quarrel."

The short trip to *The Swallow* was accomplished in silence, except for the swish of the waves past the bows and the creak of the little mast. The shallop lay low in the water because we were sixteen passengers, with baggage. I glanced over the side once, and it seemed to me that the sea looked back at me with a threatening glare. Though it was a bright, sunny afternoon, there was a special darkness in its depths, not good to see. After that I kept my eyes on the upper deck of the ship, where the passengers who were already on board were lining the rails to watch us embark.

I looked for her in vain. If I hadn't seen her go on board, I would have been afraid that she was not there. Neither Moses nor Aunt Abigail was to be seen either.

The shallop ground against the ship, which made it seem tiny by comparison. We were all helped up a rope ladder, one by one, and we climbed thankfully onto the lower deck. Andrew and I were the first up, as we had been the first to board the shallop, but we had to wait while our baggage was hauled up on a rope and dumped beside us. Still Andrew would not let me go to look for Rebecca.

"Have patience until they take the shallop aboard," he said. "After that you will be safe."

It was agony, but I followed his advice. The sailors worked fast, under the supervision of the ship's mate. They were obviously accustomed to every step of their task. Ropes were hitched around hooks at either end of the shallop, the mast was laid flat, our two sailors skipped up the ladder and went to help the others on deck who were already turning a winch. There came the shallop swinging out of the water. Everyone started back out of her way. Gradually they eased the shallop onto the blocks that were prepared for her, tying her down securely so that she would not move during the voyage.

By the time this was done, most of the passengers had gone off to find places for their baggage and to lay down their pallets. The quarrelsome Prices had scuttled away immediately, dividing their packages between them.

Andrew said, "Captain Mullins says it's every man for himself about finding a spot to sleep. I'll go and do that, while you look for the Moores."

After he had gone, I climbed to the upper deck by a narrow wooden ladder and looked about me. It seemed a huge crowd — men, women, and children, sixty or seventy at least, all taking a last, long look at the shores of

England. They were very quiet and sad-looking, standing in family groups of parents and children. Some of the women were crying, wiping their eyes surreptitiously. There was no sign of the Moores.

I went back down the ladder and through a heavy door into a long room, the full width of the ship. Bunks were built at either side, in tiers of three or four. The floor between was littered with bags and bundles of clothing, as well as sacks of food and kegs of butter and oil. Some of the bags were placed at the heads of the pallets, in the bunks, so that they couldn't be robbed while their owners slept. I had seen the same at our inn, and now indeed I recognized one or two faces from that same place.

Then, at the far end, near a tiny square window, I saw the Moores. All three were there, Rebecca looking down at her father, who was lying in the lowest bunk as if he were ill. Aunt Abigail was watching them, her hands on her hips, with an expression I had never seen on her face before. It was a mixture of exasperation and pity, and now she directed it straight at her brother. As I came closer I heard her say, "Well, brother Moses, if you intend to lie there you may starve. This is not a hospital. Every man must work to live, just as they do on land."

Moses said in a weak tone, "I'm frightened of the sea. I had no notion it's so big and so black."

"And you'll be food for the fishes in it, if you lie there like a fool," said Aunt Abigail.

"My daughter will take care of me. Rebecca will look

after me," Moses said, reaching up a hand to her and giving her his old pathetic look. "I tell you, I'm a sick man."

Where now was the confidence I had seen when he marched up from the ship this very morning? Rebecca said warmly, "Indeed, Father, I will look after you."

At that moment Aunt Abigail saw me. She let out a kind of hoot and rushed at me, grabbing my hand and pulling me forward.

"Now here's a man!" she cried out. "If you were half the man that Edward Deane is, brother Moses, you would give over your whining and stop tormenting us all."

"Edward Deane!" Moses sat up as if he had been jerked on a rope, his body suddenly filled with energy. "What are you doing here?"

"I came to be with Rebecca," I said boldly.

He gave a sharp laugh, then said, "Well, now you have your wish."

And he lay back on his pallet again and closed his eyes, as if he were asleep.

Four

IT WAS MOSES MOORE'S TERROR of the sea that made him accept me so quietly. I had expected that he would be angry, not because he loved Rebecca but because he would be afraid I would take her away from him before he was ready to part with her. Something like the reverse happened. As it turned out, he felt that another man in the party would give him protection from Aunt Abigail. He knew Rebecca would do everything she could for him, but his sister's nagging had worn him down.

As I went off to look for Andrew, Aunt Abigail came after me. She followed me out onto the lower deck and said, "I knew you were coming with us, and I said not a word."

"Rebecca told me," I said, "I'm very grateful for that."

"And now you can do something for me," she said. "Brother Moses is losing his courage. It was a miracle he ever had it, but now it's leaving him as fast as it came.

41

You must talk to him and tell him all the wonders of the New World and keep his mind on staying there. It's what he has always wanted, but I never before saw such a man for letting the good things go out of his hand."

"And yourself?" I couldn't help asking. "Did you want to go?"

"I didn't know I wanted it until Moses began to talk about it. Then I said to myself that it was better to die after one look at the wonders of the world than to live knowing every blade of grass in your own fields. I've been telling him that every day since we left Beacon, but I can see he doesn't want to hear it."

I said I thought it would be better to leave him alone for the present, that the sight of the ocean had frightened the wits out of him. I promised to do what I could for him later, when he felt better, and asked in return, "When I want to take Rebecca outside for a breath of air every day, will you make sure he lets her come with me?"

"That will be easy."

Andrew had found a resting-place for us in the stern of the ship. There was a sort of cabin there, without bunks but where our pallets and baggage could be laid, and room only for two other men. These were two brothers named Jack and Stephen Cutler, from Lincolnshire, just beyond the borders of Yorkshire. They had made several voyages to New England already and knew a great deal about it. As well as being skilled hunters, they were traders in cotton and wool, both raw and woven, small looms for weaving, fishing nets, and various other things that the settlers needed. Their sister Kate was sailing with them, but she had found a bunk in the main cabin. Kate had no reason to stay in Lincoln since their father had died, and she wanted to see the New World as her brothers had done.

I liked the Cutlers at once. They had none of the suspicious looks of the Prices, who, they said, were trading in rugs and in beads and similar things, used for barter with the Indians. Other passengers had salt, peas, flour, and meal, which they hoped to trade for furs. A man from Sussex named John White had a few she-goats and a billy in the lower hold, as well as some sheep, which the governor of New Plymouth had ordered through Captain Mullins. All of this cargo had been put on the day before we sailed.

When we had arranged our beds and piled away our property as best we could, Andrew asked, "Have you ever thought of staying in New England for good?"

Jack, the older brother, said, "Some day, maybe. Not yet. We can't afford to. For this life of trading, you must go and come with your goods or you'll never see any profit from them. There are more sharks in London waiting to eat you than in all the oceans of the world."

"Where do you stay, when you go to New England?"

"With Thomas Prence, in Plymouth. There are lodgings enough for all, houses like at home, only bigger, and they make you very welcome."

"And your sister? What will she do?"

Jack laughed and said, "If we don't watch out, she'll come hunting with us. There's nothing too hot or too heavy for Kate. But if things are going well in Plymouth, we'll leave her there and pay her a visit every time we come back from a hunting trip."

"And will you buy furs from the Indians, too?"

"As many as we can get — beaver and otter mostly. We make more out of them than out of fishing, though some believe fishing pays better in the end. It's cod mostly, the biggest you ever saw, but we don't like the smell of fish, and some captains won't let you take that cargo."

This easy, casual talk did a lot to quiet my fears. We watched the anchor being hauled in and the sails going up, and the first plunge of *The Swallow* as she set out toward the open sea. It was calm, with a tiny swell, but it seemed to me that she swished along at a great pace. I stood with my arm around Rebecca's waist, and we were both gazing back at the shores of England when Moses sidled up to me and said, "You're a good boy. Keep sister Abigail away from me and I'll never say no to you. I should have left her in Beacon. If I had known there was such a shrew lying inside her, I'd never have brought her with me."

"She means no harm," I said.

But Moses said, "Women that mean no harm are the worst. I'll promise you that Rebecca will never be like sister Abigail. Rebecca takes after her mother."

44

He rambled off then and, I suppose, went back to lie down. That was where he spent most of the voyage, in the stink and fog of the hold, with the smell of the goats and the sheep coming up through the deck from their stable below.

The very first day, while we were still in sight of land, Stephen and Jack introduced us to their sister. Kate was tall, like her brothers, with blue-black hair and dark-blue eyes. She was one of the very few passengers who looked as if she were enjoying the experience. Her eyes were dancing with excitement, and she missed nothing of what was happening. Soon she and Rebecca, who looked so different in every way, were friends.

At first the weather was fair. March, they say, is a good month for crossing the Atlantic Ocean, since the worst of the winter gales are over. But around March 21 comes the equinox, the time of year when night and day are the same length, and for some devilish reason storms come roaring like lions toward the ships.

We were ten days out when the first of these storms struck. Some of the passengers had begun to say that we would finish the crossing in a month or less. Instead of making them more civil, this notion had the effect of blowing up small quarrels into huge wars. I could only think it was because they thought they would soon get away from each other. The Prices were the worst, always ready to accuse someone of tampering with their belongings.

Boredom had something to do with it. There is nothing more boring than a long, calm voyage, if you ask me. Or so I would have said if I hadn't had Rebecca for company. We walked on the deck every morning, then found ourselves a quiet corner where we could sit and chat, while she told me what was going on in the main cabin. Where Andrew and I were lodged, with the Cutler brothers, all was peace. Usually Kate joined us, and we would spread a napkin and eat our dreadful food together as if it were a delightful feast.

Then, one night, the storm blew up. In our cramped quarters, not much more than a cupboard, suddenly it seemed that the sea was trying to get in at us through the planks of the ship's sides. It battered so loudly that it sounded like fists beating on a heavy door. It was pitch dark. I lay still, thinking I was the only one awake, until I heard Stephen say, "Here we go. It was too good to be true."

We stayed there until a little light filtered through from the deck outside. Then Stephen got up and opened the door a crack. Instantly it was wrenched out of his hand by the wind and hurled back against the frame. He reached out and pulled it closed, then said, "It's Hell let loose out there. Never saw anything like it."

Captain Mullins ordered all passengers to stay in their bunks that day. Sailors stood guard to make sure that no one came out on the deck. All sails were down and the ship was plunging along under bare poles. We peered out from time to time, risking the loss of our door. The sea was emerald green, flecked here and there with white.

The sky seemed to have disappeared. Instead we had only the sight of long, curling waves, taller and more terrible than anything I could ever have imagined. The ship climbed slowly to the tops of them, then fell shuddering down, only to begin the long crawl again. I could not believe that anything made by the hand of man could weather such a sea. A ship is only carpenter's work, after all, larchwood screwed together — how could it withstand that appalling pressure?

We tried to lie on our pallets but were constantly thrown together and away from each other with the movement of the ship. I fancied I heard wails of anguish from the other cabin. All I cared for in the whole world was there — Rebecca. It was agonizing pain not to know whether she was alive or dead. It seemed to me that the ship must sink at any moment, with all of us on board. If that was our fate, then I must meet it with her hand held in mine.

I crawled to the door. Stephen shouted above the noise of the wind, "Where are you going? You can't go out!"

But I was outside in a flash and had slammed the door shut after me. I crept along the deck like a crab, holding on to anything and everything that came to my hand. I dared not even look at the sea, which seemed to snarl louder in its anxiety to eat me up body and bones. A sailor yelled at me, "Get back! Back in there!"

I paid no heed to him. I reached the door of the big cabin and flung it open.

What a sight that was! The passengers were crouching in their bunks, visible only as little curled-up heaps in the faint light. It was like a graveyard of open graves. Were they all dead? I would have believed it but for the moans that came from them — soft, gentle, terrible moans that rose and fell with the motion of the ship. Their poor bits and pieces of property were scattered haphazard over the floor. The stench was like the worst stable I have ever smelled in my life. Most of the people were seasick and had no way to clean up and had probably stopped caring what became of them.

It was a kind of miracle that I was not seasick myself. Neither were Rebecca and Aunt Abigail, as I discovered when I reached them. But Moses was a sad sight. He was death-pale and immovable, stretched on his back with his eyes staring. Aunt Abigail had no sympathy for him, even now.

"Look at him, the hero!" she said. "Wouldn't you think his mind would be on his prayers, and we all in danger of our lives? Not him, not him. He hasn't spoken for an hour, and the last words he said were to tell me to be quiet and give over praying. A pagan, that's what he is."

Moses groaned, showing that he heard what she was saying, but I think he was past caring by now. I said, "We can pray when the storm is over. Let him be. I came to find out how you were doing."

Rebecca said, "It's terrifying. We're trapped in here. They won't let us out. How did you escape?"

"I don't know. I was just lucky. I shouldn't have done it, but I had to see you. How is Kate?"

"She has been sick, but she's beginning to feel better."

Rebecca took me to speak to her, so that I would be able to tell her brothers she was well. I had no doubt they would soon come to visit her, when they found that I had succeeded in it.

"Now that you're here," Rebecca said, "I don't feel so frightened. What is it like outside?"

"Not so bad," I said, lying boldly so that she wouldn't fear for me when I left her. "But you must not go out. You could be swept overboard. Perhaps the storm will die down soon."

Aunt Abigail said, "Can you get me some beer for these unfortunate sick people? They must have something to put the heart back into them."

I said I would try. The barrels were stored in a cubbyhole not far from the main cabin. I had been there often to collect our daily ration.

The cooper was Timothy Johnson, from Balcombe in Sussex, on the edge of Ashdown Forest. He was lonely in there by himself and was always ready for a chat. He was no more than five feet tall, but he was as wide as one of his barrels. He sat on a low stool beside them, with his eyes continually on them, as if he thought one of them might run off at any moment that he was not watching. As well as handing out beer, it was his business to make sure that the barrels didn't leak and to go over them often and caulk them if necessary. His door was hooked open as it always was. I tumbled inside and almost fell at his feet, recovering myself enough to say, "I'm sorry. Aunt Abigail asked me to come and get some beer for the sick people."

"Aunt Abigail? A genius, I can tell. Your mother's sister, or your father's?"

"Neither. She's my Rebecca's Aunt Abigail. Can you give me the beer?"

"Certainly, if you're able to carry it."

"If you have a covered can."

He had, and it was perfectly shaped for carrying in a storm, though he said it was not designed just for that. While he filled it he said, "That's a Cornish can, made of the best Cornish tin. Look how it's riveted, and the fold at the seam, to make it last. They narrow it toward the top so that it won't spill, and the lid is a fancy little cup — what more could anyone ask of a can? Now, take that to Aunt Abigail and tell her you'll go back for the can and fill it again when she has given out all that's in it."

"Is beer good for seasick people?" I asked doubtfully.

"The best. Have a drop yourself before you go."

I took a sip to please him, but I felt I was better before I drank it.

It was different with Aunt Abigail's patients, for that is what they became after I took her the first can of beer. She went like a doctor from one bunk to another, talking gently to the sick people and giving each a cupful of the beer, which certainly seemed to do them good. She broke hard bread into it and helped them to eat it. I refilled the can over and over again for her, glad of an excuse to be with Rebecca, who would not leave her father.

Before the day was over, Kate was able to help Aunt Abigail. Between them they restored some kind of order, but there was nothing they could do about the foul smell.

There were deaths, of course. Poor John White, from Sussex, was the first to go. Because of the sheep, he and I had become friendly, and I grieved for him very much. What happened was that someone got a fever, then another, until even when the storms were over and done with, the big cabin looked like a hospital.

Moses never had the fever, but he lay there moaning as if he had, just the same. I insisted that Rebecca must leave him for an hour, twice a day. He agreed to this, being thankful to me as his protector. In fact I had done nothing for him. What had happened was that Aunt Abigail was too busy with her other patients to pay much heed to him.

Once we had a calm sea again, she went herself to fetch the beer.

"A fine woman," the cooper said to me, every time I went for my own draft. "A clever woman, full of the milk of human kindness, too."

I wished that Granny Meg were with us to see the change in her. "The saint of *The Swallow*," they called her. Rebecca and Kate said that she barely slept at all but sat dozing with her lantern turned low and water simmering on her little charcoal brazier, in case anyone might need her services during the night.

When we could walk on the deck again, we drank in the blessed fresh air, and we often talked about my parents and Granny Meg. Rebecca missed Granny Meg specially, and we were both afraid she was grieving for us. Timothy Johnson, the cooper, promised that he would send a message somehow, when next he reached England. He said I could write a letter when we landed and he would take it back to England on *The Swallow*. Also, before the end of the summer other ships would come, and we should be able to find someone to take another letter home for us. Cold comfort, that was, but we were glad of the suggestion all the same.

With all sails up and a flowing sea, we made good time after the storm was over. In our little shelter, the Cutlers, Andrew, Rebecca, and I kept good health. This was partly due to Andrew's lemons, which we dipped in sugar and sucked every day. The Cutlers, being old hands, had some too. It was a soldier's trick to keep off the scurvy, they said, though usually it was only the officers who got the lemons.

If you have never been to sea, you can't possibly understand the thrill of excitement and pure joy at the first sight of land. It came in the early afternoon. The sea had been calmer for several days and a balmy breeze was blowing away all our fears and sicknesses of the mind and body. I was standing at the rail with Rebecca and thinking that if the whole voyage had been like this, it would not have been such a dreadful affair.

Suddenly I heard a long cry from the sailor in the crow's nest — a kind of basket near the top of the main-mast, where a lookout was kept day and night. It was almost a singing sound, like the call of a seabird. It brought all the sailors running, crowding together at the rails, staring ahead of the ship.

The cry came again, clearly this time, "Land — ho!"

There it was, a thin, gray line on the edge of the sea, so low that it might have been the back of a great fish. Jack Cutler was standing behind us. He said quietly, "There it is — Cape Cod. We should be able to land tomorrow."

Five

It seemed like an age before Captain Mullins would let us go ashore. That first sight we had of New England was not New Plymouth at all but a hook of land that curved around like a long arm, sheltering a half circle of water inside it. New Plymouth was beyond the fingers of the hand, and it was further sheltered by an island. Long spits of sand stretched out into the ocean, and *The Swallow* nosed her way between them at a snail's pace.

The captain seemed to regard the passengers as prisoners who would wish to escape if he took his eye off them. There was some truth in this. We were heartily sick of *The Swallow*. When we saw the sloping land out there in front of us and knew that we would soon be allowed to walk there, it was maddening to be obliged to stay on board.

We were anchored a few hundred yards off shore, not too far to see that a crowd of people was assembled, waiting for us. Behind them we could see the village, enclosed by a high palisade like a wall. On the hilltop there was a fort, with several cannon clearly to be seen. I didn't like the looks of the people on the beach. There were men, women, and children, dressed no better than they would be in England, all looking thin and hungry.

To give him his due, the captain didn't try to keep us below decks. We walked wherever we fancied, watching the cargo being unloaded, and a very interesting business it was. Our shallop was examined for leaks and then swung into the water. As soon as it was safely afloat, the sailors began to let the cargo down by means of slings worked with winches from the lower deck. They had to make a great many journeys to and from the shore, and the settlers sailed out in some of their own shallops to help them. First went the sacks — flour and beans and peas and oats — then bales of wool and cloth, then crates of household goods — pots and pans and the like — and the various things that the passengers had brought with them.

After this cargo, the animals were sent off. There were eleven sheep and a ram, and they were all terrified. They cried bitterly, as only sheep can. If John White had not died, it would have been different. When I could stand it no longer I went up to Captain Mullins and said, "I know sheep. Let me go with them."

"What do you know of them, boy?"

"My father has hundreds of them, in Yorkshire, and I would not treat one of them as you are treating these."

"What would be the difference?" he asked, sarcastically enough.

"They're afraid," I said. "They need comfort, a strong, friendly hand. They miss their shepherd. Let me take them ashore."

He let me go, though I could see he was amused that I should care so much for dumb animals. I gave my attention to the sheep only. Goats are more philosophical creatures, and when they found themselves close to the land they seemed to sense that they were safe. But the sheep were in a dreadful state. They knew me, because I had gone to take care of them every day since John White's death. They quieted down when I spoke to them. I know not what I said, but there are sounds you can make to an animal that it will understand, sounds that bring help as they would to a person in the same kind of trial.

This is why I was the first of the passengers to step ashore. Such a welcome as I got! It seemed to me that everyone came running to take my hands and ask how many were coming and if we had had a good voyage and what supplies we had brought with us. I couldn't answer half of their questions.

Then a short, red-haired man said, "Hey, you, William Clark! Show the boy where we have the pens for these beasts."

William was not much older than I was, bony and thin like the rest of the people. He led me through a gate in the palisade and showed me where the pens were and helped me to herd the sheep and goats there. The pens were well made. William said, "We're mighty glad to see you come with goats and sheep. We have been short of cheese and milk and wool. We've put a lot of work into the pens, to keep the wolves out."

He told me they had cows, brought out from Ireland, but their sheep and goats had all died last winter of some disease. I said I thought the stakes were close enough together to keep out wolves, and I asked, "Do other wild animals come?"

"Bears sometimes, foxes of course," he said. "Certain people would steal the sheep, but they're afraid of our guns."

"Do you have a gun?"

"Oh, yes," he said casually. "I wouldn't sleep without it. But the best is our cannon. We can frighten off most anyone with them. I'll show you, up on Fort Hill, a minion and a saker and two bases. We all have our orders, in case of attack."

You may be sure I was greatly alarmed at this talk, having had no idea that I was entering such a warlike community. I asked as calmly as I could, "How often do you have to turn out to fight?"

"Not for the last few months," William said cheerfully. "The sight of our pieces is enough."

He admitted that it was the men who formed the army, but boys were supposed to know the same things in case of need.

He said that he had lived in New Plymouth for nine years, having come out with his parents from London in 1624. By the time they arrived, the worst trials of the new settlement were over, houses and a few boats had been built, and most of the Indians had made peace. He threw me a glance, as if he were summing me up, then said, "What are your skills?"

"I know about sheep and goats. I can do most farming work. I know something of boatbuilding — "

"Fishing?"

"No. I only know boatbuilding because my brother is a ship carpenter, and he taught me a little of it when I stayed with him for a few weeks once. It's not much. My family lives inland, in Yorkshire."

It was enough to make people anxious to give our whole party houseroom. Strong, able-bodied people, both men and women, were what they needed. William took me back to the shore and there I met his parents, Dinah and James Clark, and his older brother Francis. Like all the older people I had seen, the Clarks looked anxious and hungry. Dinah must have been pretty once. She had beautiful reddish hair, which couldn't help curling around her ears, though she had done her best to flatten it out. Her face was deeply lined, and she looked a kindly, motherly person, rather like my own mother. The difference was that her eyes were frightened. James and Francis seemed worn and weary, though in good health.

I gave them some account of our party and where we had come from. It was then I discovered that we were the first ship to come that spring, which was why they were so very glad to see us. They knew the Cutlers, and I could see that they were well liked. They were astonished, and very pleased, at the news that Kate was in the party. About Moses Moore they asked anxiously, "Is he a skilled man, too? Can he build boats? We need house carpenters — can he do that?"

I knew not what to say. Moses had come to start a new life — it would be cruel and useless to spoil his chances before he had time to show whether or not he was able to change. Having seen how he was on the ship I had no faith in him, but I said, "Moses is as old as my father. He has experience. He has always wanted to come to New England and at last he found the courage. He is able to do all the things a farmer can do." I didn't say that he was none too willing to make a start. "And there is Andrew Hogdon — he is skilled in so many things. I could scarcely make a list of what Andrew can do."

When I came to speak of Rebecca and told them that she and I could both read and write, Dinah Clark said, "Husband, we should ask to house the Moores and this boy. The Cutlers will go to Thomas and Patience Prence's house, as they always do. Is Abigail a good housekeeper?"

"Yes," I said stoutly, "and she was the one who took care of the sick while we were at sea. She can tell at once why someone is ailing. They called her the 'saint of *The Swallow*.' I heard it myself, many times."

"You had misfortunes, then?"

"Plenty."

Dinah said to James, "Go quickly and tell Governor we'll look after them, before someone else sees them."

59

So it was arranged. When they stepped out of the shallop, Rebecca and Aunt Abigail were pleased to find that I had already found a good lodging for all of us. Andrew said in a low voice, "Well done, Edward. It's a good start. I like the look of these Clarks."

Carrying our bundles, we followed them to their house. On the way we passed a good-sized boatyard with a half-built shallop on blocks inside. A wide, clear brook ran behind the houses to our left, with a little mill wheel slowly turning. The Clarks lived in the last house on the hill, near the fort. Before taking us inside, William held me back to point out the cannon he was so proud of. They looked pretty old and rusty to me.

The house was built like an English house, a strong frame of wood with wattle and daub in between. It was surrounded by a fenced yard, where hens and chickens were pecking or resting in the dusty ground. The windows were small and high, probably because of the winds that blew in from the sea. They were closed with wooden shutters, making it very dark inside unless the door stood open.

There was one great room, which served as kitchen and living room, and four smaller rooms led off it. The hearth was at the back. A single chimney took away the smoke from the whole house. The only door faced the street. There were clean rush mats on the floor, and a neat pile of wood was stacked beside the fireplace.

We five who had been so long on *The Swallow* were

dog tired, and after a supper of bread and some boiled fowl, Andrew and Moses and I were shown a room where we could lay down our pallets. Rebecca and Aunt Abigail were given a room to themselves.

We slept like the dead until morning. I woke in the night and heard the wind rattling the roof of the house. After a moment of terror I realized that I was safe on land, and I thanked God with all my heart.

We were up and about at the dawn next day. Moses was the first, to my surprise, and I soon found out why. Before we went into the kitchen he said to me, "Now I must find the Yorkshiremen that were too saintly to have me in their company. They'll soon see that I'm as good as any of them."

"Are you sure they're here, in Plymouth?"

"Where else could they be? I'll ask around, in a crafty way, not letting people know what I'm after, just, 'I wonder if Tom Manly is still here? Or John Spindles? Or Peter Neary? Old friends of mine,' I'll say, 'from Beacon in York.' Then, when I hear where they are, I'll just walk up to them and say, 'Here I come all the way from Beacon to see how you're getting on.' And if one of them says a word against me or won't have me in their company, as not good enough, I'll have the hide off his back."

This was worse than anything I had imagined. I said, "Goodman Moore, you must not do anything violent. We're in these people's hands. They can do what they like with us. You must keep quiet and respectful."

61

"You needn't be anxious," he said calmly. "I know what I'm doing. I haven't come all this way to lift my cap to other men of my own station in life."

At first he seemed to have taken my advice. James Clark took charge of all of us the moment we appeared in the kitchen. Each family now had its own land, an acre for every member, though in the beginning they had held their land in common. James said their corn was growing well but in need of hoeing. That was the day's work, and everyone was expected to lend a hand. Andrew and Moses and one of the Clarks' servants, Paul, were to go with him. Dinah would look after Rebecca and Abigail. There was baking to do, now that the flour had come, and Dinah would show the women the wash place for the clothes, on Town Brook.

William and I were to see to the new sheep and goats and to take them and the cows to pasture. The second servant, Adam, would come with us and help to carry home the milk. The early morning was cool and we should profit from it, James said. We would come home for dinner at eleven o'clock. Tomorrow being the Sabbath, there would be no work done.

Moses took all of this very quietly, saying never a word against the plans that were being made for him. I sat at the table close beside Rebecca, watching her hands as she served the cornmeal porridge under Dinah's direction. I asked, "Is *The Swallow* all unloaded, then? Is she leaving at once?"

God knows I had never enjoyed that ship, but she was

our last link with our own country and I was loth to see
her go.

"She's unloaded, but she won't leave until she takes
on her cargo," James said. "That could take weeks. On
Monday we'll start bringing our goods to the captain,
anyone that has some to send."

"Furs?" Andrew asked.

"Plenty of them. This was a good year. Beaver and
otter are the best. They're selling now for twenty shillings
a pound. Some go in for salted and dried fish, too. We
have good saltworks at last. There's some hardwood to
go, for house carpentry and wainscoting, and staves for
barrels. They all sell well in England."

"When do you hunt and fish? In which season of the
year?"

"October to April is the season for wildfowl. Then,
when they disappear, we have fish, if we have tackle and
hawsers and nets."

"We brought some nets."

"Better than a purse of gold," James said. "With nets
we can fish for ourselves. Furs are the best. We buy from
the Indians, with cloth and beads for barter. That's the
best way. They do the work, we handle the money."

Andrew asked, "What about the Cutlers?"

I knew he had no liking for James's ideas. He would
never settle down to farming and trading. The tavern had
finished him with business.

"They're such good hunters, they do better than most.
There's not much they don't know about the wilderness

and the savages," said James. "They do their own trading. But those that go into trading only will be the richest. There isn't much money in hunting. You're not much better than the Indians. I wouldn't like it myself."

James handed Moses and Andrew a hoe each from the stock that stood against the inner wall of the kitchen. Then he led the way outside. Moses was smirking to himself, enjoying his secret plan, so clearly full of it that Aunt Abigail stopped him at the door and asked suspiciously, "What's in your mind, brother Moses?"

"Good will towards all men," said he.

Aunt Abigail said, "I hope so. Are you in good enough health to go to work?"

"Never better."

He strutted off, his hoe like a pike over his shoulder, and she went back to the house looking quite bewildered.

I spent the morning with William and asked him more questions about the family. Like myself he was the youngest. He had three sisters, all married at fifteen or sixteen years old, all with families of children. We would see them tomorrow at church and in the evening when they would come to visit their parents. His brother Francis had already been married twice, his first wife having died within a year. He had a house of his own and a son by his first marriage. William himself had what he called a precontract to marry Jane Wallis, the daughter of another trader, but they would have to wait a year because they must build a house for themselves first.

I spent most of the time until dinner with William, seeing the pasture for the cows, milking the goats and sheep and storing the milk in wooden kegs to make cheese. Twenty pints of milk went to make a cheese, he said, just as at home, and with these little animals that was a lot of milking. The sheep and goats were glad to see us and gave their milk willingly, so that I felt the morning well spent. We carried home the kegs on our shoulders and found the rest of the family assembled when we reached the Clarks' house.

I cast an eye on Moses at once and saw that his mood had changed. Gone was the air of triumph he had when I last saw him. I got Rebecca into a corner where we could not be heard and said, "Something has happened to your father. Has he spoken to you?"

"No, but I noticed it, too. He's probably tired. It's a long time since anyone put him to work with a hoe. And everything is so strange here, so different from home, it's no wonder he looks discouraged. Even I feel it's more than I can understand."

The two servants sat with us at dinner. Aunt Abigail had helped with the cooking. There were strange-looking potatoes with a sweetish taste, and buns made of cornmeal, and more beans, and slices of a huge fish that tasted almost like meat. It was a substantial meal, and it made me feel sleepy. But we had only half an hour's rest before James announced that it was time to go back to work.

The afternoon passed quietly enough, though we were all very tired by the end of it. I had thought we worked hard in Beacon, but this was something I had never seen in my life. Not a moment was wasted. Our hosts were as tired as we were, perhaps more so, but they had a dogged determination that kept them hard at work, even when good sense should have told them to stop. They seemed never to forget that their survival through the next winter depended on how well they cultivated their own plot.

I began to understand the look I had seen on their faces the day we landed. It was desperation, stark fear of starvation and failure. It was one of the ugliest sights I have ever seen in this world, yet there was a kind of grandeur about it, as if this were the most glorious choice that man could make. By comparison I felt a weakling.

Six

I WAS LOOKING FORWARD TO A GOOD REST on the Sabbath. We had slept well, better than the night before, since we were more accustomed to our surroundings. In the dawn light everything seemed intensely quiet, unnaturally still. There was not a sound from the street outside.

Dinah and James were already in the kitchen when we got there, but they gave us the shortest possible greeting. The two servants, Adam and Paul, were sitting at the table with James, who was reading aloud from a huge Bible, propped on the table in front of him. All three wore dark clothes, of a quality much better than yesterday's. William appeared a moment after us, also dressed in a handsome black suit, with black, buckled shoes.

We had put on our best, too, as we would do on Sunday at home, but we hadn't realized that we were to hold our tongues as tightly as we did. While we were eating breakfast, not a word was spoken. No one smiled. My sweet Rebecca looked sad and dispirited. William was like an old man. Andrew made to speak once or twice but decided against it. Aunt Abigail took her cue from Dinah and looked more pious than I had ever seen her in my life.

The most pitiful of all was poor Moses. He glanced at the Bible and away again, as if he had never seen one before. He gave a long, noisy sigh, turned it into a cough, then sighed again, tried to catch Aunt Abigail's eye but gave up the effort, and at last fixed his gaze on the table so firmly that he seemed not to notice when Rebecca put a plate of cornmeal porridge in front of him. I felt a sharp inclination to giggle like a little girl, but I made sure to keep as gloomy a face as the rest of them. Solemn behavior always has a bad effect on me.

There was more to come. While we sat in total silence, we heard a drum begin to beat in the street outside. James stood up, fetched his musket from its place in the corner and said, "Time to be off. Everyone takes his gun."

William and the two servants took one each from the same stack, and Andrew and I went to our room to get ours and one for Moses. Then we followed James outside.

It was a beautiful sunny day, with a gentle breeze. As we walked down the hill we could see *The Swallow* riding at anchor offshore, but there was no sign of life on her that we could see.

At the foot of the street a crowd of men was already assembled, each with his musket on his shoulder. They were all wearing good cloaks and dark suits with white linen stockings. As they formed themselves three abreast, the drummer ceased and a uniformed sergeant stepped out in front. Off we went, marching briskly up the street, past the Clarks' house again, until we reached the fort.

Andrew marched between James and Moses. Then came the Cutlers and Captain Mullins, with a few of his crew. Timothy Johnson, the cooper, was there, looking as cheerful as ever, and most of the passengers who had come on *The Swallow*. I saw no sign of the Prices, though I looked about for them.

William and I joined in at the back, for which I was glad, as he told me the names of the different notabilities. Behind us came Governor Bradford in his long robe, with Mr. Ralph Smith, the pastor, also in a cloak, on his right. William whispered that Pastor Smith was a very learned man, of Saint Peter's College in Cambridge University. To Master Bradford's left came Captain Myles Standish, the little red-haired man who had sent me off with William the first day. He looked much more dignified now, with a cloak like the rest but wearing his side arms and carrying a small cane in his hand, as a sign of his office, I suppose.

The whole procession marched into the meetinghouse of the fort, which served as a church as well. The men filled the seats at the right-hand side. I noticed that they set down their arms beside them, as if they expected to have to use them during the service. I wondered if they had once been attacked while they were in there at their prayers.

We waited in solemn silence until there was a rustle outside and the women and children began to arrive. The women took the left-hand side, and the children were all herded into a kind of pen at the back by two stout matrons armed with long sticks.

The pastor mounted a low platform at the top of the room and opened a huge Bible that was laid on a table in front of him. When the congregation was settled, he began, "In the name of God, Amen."

The opening prayer lasted at least an hour. Mr. Smith gave thanks for our safe passage, and for the good things we had brought with us, and for our eager spirit that would keep us working day and night for the greater good of all. Then there was prayer for the recalcitrant and the hard of heart, and for the sinners who tried to cheat their neighbors and the community, and who would certainly pay for it both now and on the Day of Judgment. All of this was sprinkled with words and phrases in Greek and Latin, which the people seemed specially to enjoy, though I could have sworn they knew as little of those languages as I did.

After the prayer we had a long passage from the Bible, on which the pastor commented as he went along. It was about Noah and the great flood and the terrors and dangers of traveling by sea. That kept him going for another hour.

When he paused, everyone stood up and I thought we were going to be released at last. But it was only for some hymns, which were sung in such a screechy way that there was no pleasure in it. I always loved to sing in church, but these hymns were strange to me. Besides, everyone looked so glum that I began to think they found it all as nasty as I did. I even wondered if they did it like that specially to mortify the flesh.

After the singing, we sat down for another sermon and some more prayers, until it seemed that Mr. Smith himself must be bone weary, as I was. Throughout the three hours of the service, the two stout women used their sticks frequently on any child who moved, so that the religious discourse was punctuated with yelps of pain.

Moses was sitting just in front of me. I soon noticed that his eyes were searching the congregation anxiously, in hope and then in despair.

At last the pastor came to a stop, his voice creaking with exhaustion.

"And so, my friends," he said wearily, "every jot and tittle of our lives will be taken into account, every divilish error, every divine truth, every false statement, every light word, every good deed, every evil action, until the dread Day of Judgment comes upon us. Then it will be decided once and for all time whether we go to our reward in Heaven or burn forever in the everlasting pains of Hell."

In perfect silence we all trooped outside and started for home, our hearts as heavy as lead.

That was a gloomy Sabbath day, if ever I saw one. Dinner was not as silent as breakfast, but there was an air of hurry about it since we had another three-hour session in church right after it. During the second one, again Moses sat with me, and I saw how his head went lower and lower on his chest as the hours went on.

I had not expected anything good of the second service, but it turned out to be much more interesting than the morning one. First Deacon Fuller read a piece from the letter of Saint Paul, on charity. He gave a short homily on it and was followed by Pastor Smith with some more. After him the governor spoke. He seemed a kindly, gentle man, but there was something frightening about him just the same. When he had finished, the deacon said, "Now we will hear the voice of any man who feels the spirit of God moving him to prophecy."

There was a long pause, until one after another the men began to speak about what charity meant to them, how they ruled their lives by it, how they would exhort people who failed in it. They gave examples of times when charity had been almost too difficult, but when perseverance had led to success. I tried to imagine our parson in Beacon allowing us to speak up like this, but it was impossible. I thought it a very good thing, in that it gave people a better chance of knowing each other.

At last Deacon Fuller stood up again and said, "Now I take leave to remind every man present of his duty to contribute what he can to the upkeep of our church and its pastors."

Beginning with the governor, all the men walked down to where the deacon stood with his bag, dropped something in, and returned to their seats. Then there was a final prayer and we all shuffled outside.

I could not make out which of the older residents were Moses's old friends from Beacon. None of them seemed to take any notice of him. If he had already insulted them, as he had planned to do, surely they would have spoken of it during the time of prophecy.

On the way home I found out what had happened. I made sure to walk with Moses, who was shambling along with his head down, a shadow of the man who had set out with his hoe over his shoulder only yesterday.

"Goodman Moore," I said, "are you sick? What has happened to you? Yesterday you were in such good fettle."

"Not sick, Edward," he said. "I've come all this way to pull the whiskers of my three old neighbors, and there isn't a single one of them here to say me no."

I had no inclination to laugh, he sounded so dreadfully sad. I asked, "Why? Where are they?"

"Under the green sod, boy," he said. "Dead and gone, this five or six years. I asked everyone I saw yesterday, and that was the news they gave me. Dead and gone. I still had hopes until today that I would see them, that I was told wrong, and that they would march to the church with the rest of us, but there was never a sign of them. And I came all the way across the wide ocean to see them. Dead and gone."

He made it sound as if he had taken the journey purely

out of love for his old friends, though both of us knew that this was very far from the truth.

The evening was pleasanter than I had expected. The married daughters of the Clarks came to visit, with their children, and William's future wife, Jane. The Cutlers came, too, with Kate, bringing two young men who were friends of theirs. I noticed that Andrew made sure to sit as close to Kate as possible. This was quite troublesome for him; I suspected that the young men had been told that two lovely young girls had arrived and were there to view them. One of them was watching Rebecca, which made me furious.

Kate and Rebecca helped Dinah to serve supper, and now we had beer with it, a great change for the better. The men became more cheerful and began to tell stories.

That was when we heard most about the early years of the settlement. My skin crawled as they talked of starvation and of trying to live on shellfish and of their first friendship with the Indian, Squanto, long since dead of what they called the Indian sickness. Squanto knew some English, which he had learned from earlier settlers, and he was able to interpret for them so that they could begin trading with the Indians.

Because of the new audience, more and more stories came out. They told us that the first people to arrive from England had found not a soul alive on Cape Cod, nor at Plymouth, though they saw small bands of Indians from time to time. It was Squanto who told them that the whole tribe who lived on that coast was wiped out by sickness, the very winter before. Were it not for the corn those poor people had saved in pits, the men who were telling us of it would have died of starvation themselves.

The three sons-in-law, Isaac and Samuel and Richard, were only children then, but they remembered it vividly. Both had come over from England with their parents and had seen them die the very first winter. They had been taken in by other families and brought up by them as their own.

Gradually the people had built houses and the great palisade that surrounded their village and had set up trading posts up north to buy furs from the Indian hunters. The newest one was inland to the west, along a broad river on which the Indians transported the furs in canoes. Throughout the spring and summer, when the ships came out from England, they traded these for gunpowder and shot, fishing tackle and nets, nails and screws, clothing of all kinds, and the peas and beans that they had still not managed to grow themselves.

"God was with us," James Clark said. "Many a time we were near to perishing, but we were always saved in the nick of time. Every man knows that his duty is to plant the Gospel in this remote and barbarous wilderness and edify the poor savages with our wise and godly behavior. Satan is always busy, even among our company. Opposers are not wanting. In every way we strive to pacify the wrath of the Lord by humbling ourselves before him."

Everyone murmured agreement. I never saw such a

serious, truly religious group of people in all my life, yet it was soon obvious that things other than religion were also on their minds.

Only two years before, no less than ten ships had arrived from England, crammed with people just as godly as our hosts, all fleeing from persecution of their religion in England. Some had settled farther north in Massachusetts, and some had gone to Charlestown in Virginia. The northern settlers were trading in furs, too, and were competing with the Plymouth ones. No one could tell what the result would be. Those who had gone south had suffered great sickness and many of them had died, so there was little to fear from them.

Aunt Abigail sat with Dinah, drinking in every word, moving her gaze from one speaker to another as if she had never heard such wisdom in all her life, nodding her head forcefully at every pious sentiment. Moses was a different story. The beer had begun to rise in his head, and he was summoning the courage to speak. As the visitors stood up to go home he said, "If you want to bring God to the savages, why were there none of them in the church?"

James turned a look of displeasure on him, then said, "Because they will not come. They still live in the darkness of paganism and ignorance. We know not the Lord's plans for them, but we hope in time that they will come to us of their own free will. That is the way for the truly repentant sinner."

James didn't seem to hold Moses's question against

him, but he clearly included him among those who had not yet repented.

Moses suffered only ten more days of hoeing before he rebelled. What finished him was the service that we were obliged to attend every Thursday evening. It was called a lecture, but it was not much different from the Sunday afternoon service. Most of the time was given to Bible reading and comments from the congregation and from Pastor Smith. And it was every bit as long.

The law of the settlement decreed that everyone who wished to have a say in the affairs of the town was obliged to attend the services, unless he was sick in bed. Those who didn't go to church were tolerated for the work they did, but they were ranked as mere servants and never consulted on important questions. Jack Cutler explained this to us, and he said, "If you mean to live here, it would be better to keep to their rules. We always go to services when we're in town. That way we get a good welcome when we come back from a trip."

Andrew thought this a good policy, as he had no wish to offend the people of Plymouth, but he agreed with me that their idea of religion was too far from the Church of England to make us want to change. At home we were churchgoing folk, without asking too many questions, and to please Parson, and because we believed in God and Heaven and Hell.

For myself, I was glad of a rest at church time, and after a while I began to suspect that many of the people felt the same. It was good to dress in clean clothes on

Thursdays and sit quietly for a few hours, instead of mucking out stables as I had to do at this time every other evening except Sunday.

The drawback was that the hour after work was the only time when Rebecca and I could be together, making plans for our marriage and saying all the sweet things that lovers say. There could be mighty little of that on Thursdays, and none on Sundays. Andrew was restless, too, but he was satisfied for the moment to be able to watch Kate where she sat with the women, even if he could not speak to her.

On the second Friday morning, when we had been there two weeks, just before dinnertime, I was bringing home the milk churns with Adam and William when I saw Moses come marching from the direction of the cornfield. There was no sign of his hoe. I asked quickly, "What's happened? Why have you come home so early?"

"That man, Clark, he thinks I'm a dog. Orders here, orders there, do this, do that — I've had enough of it. I'm off to the tavern for a mug of beer, to wash out the taste of his talk."

I had seen the tavern close by the shore, but James Clark spoke of it as if it were the home of Satan himself. It was used mostly by sailors and fishermen and trappers back from the wilds.

"Does Master Clark know you've left the field?" I said.

"He may know or he may not. If he's not blind, he

saw me throw down my hoe. Mind you, I said nothing. Working like a horse, like a dog, like a. . . ."

His ideas of work gave out then. He marched ahead of me into the house and shouted at Aunt Abigail, "Give me my dinner, woman, and let me be going."

"Where will you go, you godless heathen?" she demanded.

Dinah stood by with a long spoon in her hand, watching them, her eyes on pins, as we say.

Rebecca ran forward crying, "Father, what has happened? Are you sick?"

"Alive and well is what I am. I'm taking no more orders from anyone. I've worked all my life and now, when I'm old, I can have my rest. I'm sick and tired of hearing about my last end. If that comes, I'll face it, but I'm not hurrying to meet it, like some I know."

Rebecca could not have brought herself to question that statement, but Aunt Abigail did.

"Work?" she said. "When did you work? It must have been before I was born. I never saw you work in all my life. The first time that you're asked to do a hand's turn, you start yelling about all the work you've done. How do you think people can live without work?"

"Some live very well," he said. "I have some of my own money still, and I'll live on that. I have friends. I don't have to bow and scrape and moan to get a plate of porridge or a bowl of soup. No one ever prayed over me in this world, and I won't stand it now."

"Who prayed over you? What are you talking about?"

"Master Clark prayed over me, down in the field. He stood there, holding up his hoe to heaven, asking God to send down a voice to tell me to get on faster with the work."

Aunt Abigail burst out laughing, then said, "I never thought of doing that."

Moses clenched his fists and leaned suddenly toward her, as if he were going to strike her. Then he thought better of it.

"Here I am," he said, "lost in a far country, all my friends dead and gone. Why should I listen to orders at my time of life?"

"All right, all right," Aunt Abigail said. "You've told us that already. Here's your dinner. Eat it up, for the love of God, and be gone out of the house before the rest of the people come home. Am I not right, Dinah?"

"Yes, yes," she said, "get him gone before James comes home. I thought he was a good, honest man, sister Abigail. I liked the looks of him. I had no idea — no idea — "

"Now, sister Dinah, don't cry," said Abigail. "Moses is all right as long as he gets his own way."

So he got his way. They fed him and sped him out of the house before the rest of the party came home to dinner. He had said he would go to the tavern, and that was indeed where he went.

Some time in the middle of the night, there came Moses, singing at the top of his voice, cursing and swearing fit to make anyone even less than a Saint blush, crawling into his bed and snoring like a trooper all night long.

The next day he had a fearful headache, and he was rather inclined to regret what he had done. At breakfast he said, "Master Clark, I'm sorry I'm not the man you thought I was. I'm sorry indeed. You and I will both be glad if I move off somewhere else and leave you in peace."

James said in a tight voice, "No, brother Moses, we long for you to repent and join the brethren of the Lord."

"It's no use," Moses said. "I'm not fit. I'd best be going. I'll leave you my daughter, to your help and to her protection, but I can't stay with you any longer."

Rebecca asked, "And where will you live, in this wild country? Can I not come with you to look after your house?"

"Don't worry, girl," Moses said. "I'll be in good hands. You couldn't live where I'll be."

"Where is that?" Abigail demanded.

"With the Prices. They have a place back in the woods. They said I'll be welcome."

"The Prices! Those godless, thievish brothers that never darken the door of the church, that live heathenish lives of — of — "

Words failed James. He bowed his head and said no more.

Aunt Abigail was the only one who refused to be worried about Moses.

"Go, then," she said. "Go. See how you like it without your comfort. When you begin to miss it, you can come home to us here and we'll take you in, in the Christian spirit. When you get hungry and there isn't a bite to eat in the house, you may remember the friends you left behind."

Seven

The Swallow WAS LADEN IN A MONTH, and as the time for her departure approached, Rebecca and I wrote a letter to my parents and to Granny Meg. Timothy Johnson promised to carry it. He said he would see to it that our letter reached Beacon within two weeks of his arrival at home.

We had become very fond of him, and so had Dinah Clark. Whenever he had a chance, he came ashore with *The Swallow*'s shallop and walked up to sit in the kitchen in the evening. He liked going to sea, he said, but he had promised his wife that this voyage would be his last. Dinah said more than once, "Would you not stay with us here? Send for your wife and children and come to live in New Plymouth? There is plenty of work here for a cooper, not just barrels for beer and wine but hogsheads for the furs as well. You might make your fortune."

But Timothy was not to be persuaded. He would end his days in Balcombe on dry land, he said, working at the brewery where his father had worked before him.

James had some paper and a bottle of dried-up ink, which we watered until it could be used. Then we cut a pen each from the bunch of goose feathers that were used to sweep the ashes on the hearth. Dinah watched us in wonder as we sat down together to write the letter. I began it.

We are both well and are settled in the New Plymouth with very good people, Master James Clark and his wife Dinah. We had a good voyage, though there was a bad storm, but praise be to God we are all safe. This is a beautiful country and the people are very prosperous and happy. We have seen no wolves, though we sometimes hear the foxes bark by night, like ours. It makes us think of home. We have heard that there are bears and wolves and beavers and otters, which the people catch for their furs. They get very rich and do business with the Indians for furs and other things. We will be married in a year or so, when we have built a house to live in. We hope to be able to write to you again before the end of the summer while the ships are still running. In winter no one comes here, no one at all.

Rebecca added a piece of her own:

I wish we could see you, Granny Meg, just that I could run in and out of the kitchen as I always did.

Here I am a grown woman, with a great deal of work to do.

We thought it better not to give any news of Moses, since we could tell nothing good of him, but Rebecca added to her piece that Aunt Abigail was well and liking New England very much.

We folded the letter and gave it to Timothy on the night before he left. He looked at us sadly and said, "I wonder when I'll see you again. Take good care of your girl, Edward. I have never seen one like her."

Next morning we joined the great crowd on the shore that had come to watch *The Swallow* sail off. She was well loaded with goods, which the captain said would fetch a proper price in London. He thought he might not be able to come again before the winter set in, but he promised to bring out things that we would need at the earliest possible date in the spring. Everyone trusted Captain Mullins, and they said as much when he was gone. Deacon Fuller said, "If all were like that good, honest man, we would never fear for our lives when winter comes."

I liked not this talk of winter. Every day we heard something of it, though it was high summer and we had enough and to spare for living.

As soon as *The Swallow* was gone, I was put to work at building a shallop to be used for fishing. It was well for me that some of the other men knew the skills of boatbuilding, for my knowledge was not equal to theirs. On the day we landed I had felt confident enough, but faced with a pile of timber and a saw, with no one to give any orders but myself, I would have made a sad mess of it.

I tried not to show my ignorance, however, and in fact I learned that I could add to my knowledge quietly, so that in the end I turned out very good work. Even if I had been an expert, I would not have known the needs of boats in those turbulent waters. A boat must always be constructed to suit the conditions in which she will sail, and these had been discovered by the men who had lived in New Plymouth for almost twelve years. They were still a great mystery to me.

Even while the shallop was building, as far as possible I avoided going to sea. I had had enough of sailing during our voyage. The other men were pleased enough to let me stay at home when they went fishing, since there was one less to divide the catch.

Life was quieter and better without Moses. Aunt Abigail had no fears for him. She said over and over, "Moses never comes to any harm. You'll see that he'll turn up one of these days with his tail between his legs, expecting us to forget all his adventures."

The next to leave us was Andrew. He came in one evening and said, "Autumn is coming on and the Cutlers will soon go hunting. I'll be with them."

"Where? Where will you go?"

"I'll follow them. They know where the best hunting

is. I want to see the wild country to the west, where no one but the Indians has ever walked."

"What about Kate?"

"She must wait until I come back. Take care of her."

This was what Timothy had said to me about Rebecca. There was no contract between Andrew and Kate that I had heard, but we could see that she was sad when he went. She spent a lot of time at the Clark's house talking to Rebecca while they got on with their spinning, when I and all the men were out at work.

There was no sign of Moses. We heard that he went trapping with the Prices, living out in the woods for a while and bringing home their furs now and then. Sometimes they came roaring into town and drank at the tavern, until the owner was warned not to serve them again. After that they must have found another place to go, for no one saw them for weeks at a time.

We could do nothing. I went to look for him once, finding the house with great difficulty. It was set at the end of an overgrown track through the woods. Tall weeds grew up to the very door and looked in through the torn windows. The house had been strongly built once, but it was so neglected that there were holes in the walls where the plaster had fallen out.

Inside it was more like an animal's lair than a house for human beings. There was no one at home except a mongrel dog that growled at me viciously. It was lying on a heap of rags in the corner of the room. It half rose to threaten me, showing its teeth. I backed out again very quickly, not only to escape the dog but because of the stench of rotting furs that filled the air so that one dared not breathe it in.

Furs lay everywhere, in heaps on the floor and on racks that hung from the rafters, where they swung in the breeze that blew through the window openings and the gaps in the walls. They should have been worth a small fortune, as I already knew from listening to the men's talk, but so many of these were rotting away and so many were being eaten by all kinds of insects that I couldn't imagine their value being high when the time came to sell them.

The notion of Moses off trapping in the woods was as hard to imagine as Moses with a hoe in his hand going to work in the cornfield. I had seen that wonder and was prepared to believe in the other.

Perhaps this was why I told Rebecca later, "I've seen where your father lives, and it's not so bad. It may be that he'll succeed well after all."

"Do you think I should go there and keep house for him?"

"No. He doesn't want it. Besides, there are the Prices. They all live together, don't forget. There would be no place for you."

The suggestion had put me in a panic, as may be imagined. She took my advice and promised to wait and see what Moses would do next.

It was not long before we knew most of the people of Plymouth either by name or by sight. Mr. Smith, the pastor, was a man too great to speak to us, except in a kindly way when we met after church on Sundays. His new helper, the man they called their teacher, was more friendly and full of life and much younger, as well. His name was Roger Williams. He had come from Salem to New Plymouth a week or two after we had. He was not a solemn person like the older Saints, Governor Bradford and Deacon Fuller and the rest.

This was why I was not afraid of him when he stopped me one day as I was going down to the boatyard and said, "Edward Deane, may I have a word with you?"

"Surely."

"Come and sit with me. I have to ask a favor of you."

He led me into his house nearby. I had never been inside it before. It was small but so neat that it looked bigger. The first room just off the street was his study, where he had his desk and his books. Through the open door I could see the kitchen, with his garden beyond. I had often noticed him working there when I passed by, since like the rest of us he had to cultivate whatever food he needed for himself and his family.

"You like my books," he said, seeing me glance at them more than once. "I've heard that you can read and write."

"Yes. Deacon Graves of Beacon taught me, and I taught Rebecca Moore."

"I was told that she can read, too. I want to ask if you would both teach school for us here in Plymouth."

I had never thought of such a thing, though I knew

that no one was teaching the children to read, unless their parents were able to do it. Most of them were too busy to give their time to that, no more than they could have done it at home in Beacon. But there we always had our deacon, and while he had his little school no one needed to be illiterate.

"Am I not too ignorant?" I said.

"So are the children. You have some books."

I couldn't understand how he knew that, unless the Clarks had told him.

"I have only three books," I said.

"What are they?"

"*Reading and Writing, Simple Arithmetic,* and *The Practice of Medicine.*"

"The start of a good library. I can lend you more, if you want to study. Governor Bradford is very anxious for you to undertake this work. He will give a room in his house for it."

"Governor Bradford!"

I had never dreamed of such a high position, but remembering the boatbuilding and how I had progressed at that, I said, "Of course I will do it. But Rebecca must be with me. Either of us alone would founder. Together we might make a fair hand of it."

"We'll consult the governor about that. I'll try to persuade him to agree to it."

"Do you think he might not?"

"He has a very tender conscience in some matters," Master Williams said sardonically.

I knew not what to answer to this. I had never before heard anyone speak other than in praise of the governor, though there were several things I disagreed with myself, such as his idea that people who didn't go to all the church services should be put in the stocks. And I had seen a young man and his wife in the stocks because their first baby was born eight months after their wedding, and the Elders decided that they had committed sin before the date of their marriage. They swore that it was not so, but the husband was beaten and both of them disgraced just the same.

I had promised Andrew that I would not complain aloud of anything in New Plymouth until his return. I was anxious to keep to this now, but Master Williams said, "You are newly out from England, and there are things here that must go against your conscience. Some of them certainly go against mine. How can we know the designs of God unless we continue to be seekers after the truth? I will always be a seeker. Some of the Saints are certain that they have found the one truth already, and they don't wish for any more to be added to it. They want everyone to accept the version that they believe, and they will allow no one to question them. Have you not seen that?"

"I have seen it," I said reluctantly, "but I've decided to keep my own counsel. I would be a seeker, too, if I could, but I may never find the great truth."

"Everyone who seeks earnestly will find it, sooner or later. Otherwise how can it be the truth? It will not be the same for everyone, or at least it will show itself in different ways. I have not said much of this to Master Bradford, but enough for him to say that I have a windmill in my head. I am glad of the windmill, if it leads me closer to the love of God and man. It's that windmill that sends me among the Indians, into their filthy huts, to make friends with them and bring them to God."

"Why has Governor Bradford chosen me, if he suspects that I'm not converted?"

"There is no one else, and besides he does not suspect it. These are only thoughts that came to me when I saw you looking at my books."

That same evening, Governor Bradford sent for Rebecca to come to his house. As it was already dark, I went with her. There we found Master Brewster, the most important of the Elders, sitting with Master Bradford. They received us very kindly, making us sit down with them and offering us nuts and beer. Master Bradford was worried about Rebecca's being able to read and questioned her very closely about it, saying, "Why were you not content to do women's things, spinning and sewing and cooking and the like?"

"I can do those things, too," she said quietly. "Mistress Clark will tell you."

"She has told me. But this reading — doesn't it distract your mind from a woman's duties?"

"I think it improves them," she said. "It gives me thoughts that I would never have otherwise, while I do mechanical things."

I could see that they were taken with her, but the governor remained in doubt about the effect of reading on a woman's mind. Though he didn't say so precisely, his main fear seemed to be that other women would want to read, too, and that what they learned would teach them to rebel against the order that was laid down for them.

When we came to open the school, the little girls were not allowed to come with their brothers, even if there was no work for them at home. We cut slates and soon had more than twenty boys of all ages scratching the letter A, big and small, in lines across them. Rebecca did most of the teaching, since between the boatbuilding, the sheep and cattle, and all my other chores I had already too much on my hands. Often I had to leave her alone to supervise the lessons while I attended to these things.

One day, when we were no more than halfway through the alphabet, I came back to the school just before dinner to help Rebecca collect the slates and put them away. There, sitting at the back of the room, with a slate on her knee and a chip of sharp stone in her hand, working as hard as any of the children, was Aunt Abigail. I leaned over her shoulder and corrected the shape of her letter K.

"Drat!" she said. "I always get that one wrong."

As she had only begun that morning, some of her other letters were copied wrong, too. She had been working at it for two hours, Rebecca said, and was learning faster than anyone in the room. She stayed to help us clear up, and I said, "I didn't know you were interested in learning to read, Aunt Abigail."

"It's that other book you have," she said. "I want to be able to read it."

"My other book?"

"Yes. The one about diseases and cures. From what I can hear, I'm going to be glad of what's in that book before very long."

"What do you mean?"

"You'll see, when winter comes."

From then onward, I read my *Practice of Medicine* to her each evening. By day she struggled with her letters and tried to spell out the words by herself. James was worried about this at first, but when I reminded him that Aunt Abigail had proved her skill on *The Swallow*, he said no more.

When she had time, she went to the woods and picked various herbs that the book recommended, as well as strawberry leaves and sassafras, which she boiled up with sugar to make a syrup. This was what Deacon Fuller advised her to do. He was the settlement's only doctor, and he showed her a great many of his own herbs and cures. Until he took an interest in her studies, one or two people had murmured that she might be a witch. Her friendship with Deacon Fuller put a stop to that.

With the first frost in late September, the trees began to turn gold and orange and brown. From the hilltop above New Plymouth the forest was a sea of all these colors, flecked with a dozen shades of green.

Preparations began for the harvest festival. The men went off before dawn every morning to shoot wild duck and turkey. Every house fluttered with goose and chicken feathers. Carcasses of deer hung in the larders, and the hunters had long discussions about the best way to carve them for cooking. William's future father-in-law, Jacob Wallis, never ceased to enjoy his freedom to hunt.

"At home in Sussex," he said to me, "if I shot a deer I'd be hanged for it. God had made a present of them all to the duke. Here they would be more likely to hang me for not shooting enough of them."

Dinah and Rebecca made corn bread and white bread and pancakes and cooked wild plums and grapes in red wine and spices. There were pickled eels and clams and some small shellfish that tasted almost sweet.

The holiday lasted three days. It began with a service in the Common House and a review of Captain Standish's army in their red coats. A great many Indians came into town, wearing deerskins now because of the cold weather. They were entertained by the governor and the elders in their houses. The other families moved from one house to another among their kin, each time finding a huge spread laid out, with plenty of strong red wine. After dinner we had games and sports, just as at home.

With us, the first feast was at the Clarks'. Then we went to the Wallises' and on the third day to Francis's house, where his wife Prudence had the last and the best feast of all. Francis was very proud of her and kept telling us to try more and more of her cakes and pies, which we were very willing to do.

The last of the ships hurried away and soon the October gales were blowing like mad along that wild, rough coast. Fences came down and roofs were carried away. For days on end no one could go outside the door without being swept along by the wind. The sheep and cattle had to be penned all the time, and they wailed miserably, hating their confinement as much as we did.

When the first storms died down, the snow came. One morning we looked out to find that the whole world was silent and white and desolate. The boats were safely drawn up and sheltered as well as possible with wicker covers. We had stocks of hay for the sheep and cattle. Our stores were full of root vegetables, sacks of corn and flour, dried and salted fish, and salted meat for special occasions. James and Dinah said that there would be enough.

Then, late in the afternoon, when we were sitting down to supper, there was a thump on the door, as if someone had hit it with his fist. James went to open it, and Moses Moore almost fell into the room.

Eight

FOR A MOMENT NONE OF US RECOGNIZED HIM. It's true that I had been thinking of him all day, since I had seen the snow, wondering how he was faring in his shack in the woods, but I could never have imagined him as he looked to us now. His clothes were covered in snow so that he was a shapeless mass of feathery white, like a goose. His beard was frosted and had clearly not been trimmed for a long time. Worst of all were his eyes, frightened, almost demented, as if he had been followed to our door by wolves.

Rebecca was on her knees beside him in a second, trying to lift him up, crying out, "Father, Father, what has happened? Where have you been?"

William and I got him upright between us and led him toward the fire, where James was placing his own big rocking chair close to the blazing logs.

Aunt Abigail warned, "Not too close. If he's frostbitten he must be warmed little by little."

97

We eased him into the chair and Rebecca took off his broken boots and stockings, which seemed not to have been removed for weeks. Then she brought a basin and warm water and made him put his feet in it and took off his jacket and muffler, wrapping him in a rug instead. Meanwhile Dinah was heating soup in a little pot at the fire. Rebecca fed it to him by tiny spoonfuls, until he began to show some signs of recovery.

The first one was that he put out his hand and stroked her arm, in a way that I had never imagined he could do. His voice was a bare whisper when he said, "A good girl always, like your mother."

We got him into bed after a while, with hot stones wrapped in flannel at his feet and plenty of blankets. The look of wonder on his face was a sight to see, but he scarcely spoke at all, only looked from one of us to the other as if he had never seen our faces before.

He stayed in bed for several days, scarcely moving at all, swallowing everything he was given. James trimmed his beard and hair for him so that he looked less of a fright than when we had seen him first.

Apart from that, Aunt Abigail took charge of him herself, since the rest of us had so much to do. The animals had to be fed and watered every day, the cows and goats milked, and the milk that we didn't use ourselves taken to the central barrels to be made into butter and cheese. Just as at home, various repairs had been left for the winter — new handles fitted to spades and hoes, damaged sickles ground down by the blacksmith — all the small things that we could never take time for in good weather.

The snow melted in a few days and we were able to move around again, but it was bitter cold. Even the sea froze solid, and the ground under our feet was as hard as iron. Still it was good to be able to go outside again, though I was warned to keep my mouth and nose covered with a muffler.

Perhaps that was an exceptionally hard winter. Whatever it was, I hope never to see another like it. I thought often of my mother and her complaints against the cold of Yorkshire. I would not be able to describe to her what this was like — there are not enough words in our language for it.

Aunt Abigail seemed to thrive on it. She put on an extra petticoat, but otherwise you would think she was at home in England. I couldn't believe she was the same person who used to come whining to Granny Meg with her troubles.

The difference was that here in New England the boot was on the other foot. People came for advice to her. Whether she was going in and out to the chickens, spinning or knitting by the fire, or helping Dinah with the cooking, she was always ready to drop everything and hold a conference with a patient. They would sit together at the kitchen table, with my book between them, and Aunt Abigail would turn the pages slowly and solemnly. The visitor would wait anxiously, until at last she would close the book and announce her remedy.

The rest of us tried to keep out of the kitchen while this was going on, so that the patient could describe his or her ailment in privacy. As many men as women came to consult her, especially when Deacon Fuller was away. Since he was often summoned to quite distant places, he was glad to have a substitute to take over for him sometimes.

I knew that Aunt Abigail could read only the parts of the book that we had gone over often together, but one would never guess it from watching her. She had learned these parts by heart, and she was gradually adding to her knowledge. Deacon Fuller's syrup was her great standby, for colds and stomachaches and fevers, but the recipes for cures that were given in the book were a great help to her as well. Some she would not use, like mouse's dung for sick children, but she had great faith in a draft of the husband's urine for fever after childbirth.

Often she had to leave the house to go and visit her patients at home. She never took the book with her then, lest it might come to some harm.

When the snow was gone, one day Moses struggled out of bed and came to sit by the kitchen fire. He was barely able to walk. James and I took one arm each, and we got him into the rocking chair. Then James put extra logs on the fire and settled a rug around his feet, saying, "Now, old friend, you're snug enough. Some strong waters every evening with sugar, and soon you'll be as good as new."

Moses huddled in his rug, looking up at him sadly. At last he said, "Brother James, you are a good man. I left your house in a fit of anger, and still you have treated me kindly when I had to come crawling back to you."

"A good Christian is always ready to receive the repentant sinner," said James.

I caught Rebecca's eyes over their heads and saw the terror in them. I was in a panic myself. Moses had marched out in fury when James prayed over him in the field. So far as we knew, he was not the man to let himself be described as a sinner, repentant or not. But to our amazement all he said was, "A good Christian indeed."

Moses enjoyed the new life that Aunt Abigail's medical practice brought to the house. As an invalid himself, he was full of sympathy for the people who came to see her, and if she was not at home when they arrived he would entertain them happily with an account of his own symptoms, as well as listening to theirs.

He kept very quiet in Aunt Abigail's presence, however. I guessed that he didn't want to draw her attention on himself, lest she might think it was time he went back to work. In fact she continued to take good care of him. She saw that he ate well, and she helped him to move his frostbitten feet a little every day, in the hope that life would come back to them.

William was a handy carpenter, and after a while he made Moses a pair of crutches. He learned to hobble about on them, so that he was not entirely helpless, but it was plain to all of us that he would never again be the man he was when he came to New Plymouth in the spring.

When the first shock of the cold weather was over, I found that I was better able to stand it. There were warmer spells sometimes, though not for long. William began to build a house for himself and Jane, and I spent as much time as I could helping him with it. Paul and Adam did the heavy work of hauling the wood for the roof and the walls.

Adam was a Devon man, but he said he had no reason ever to go back there. He had great plans to make his fortune as soon as his time was up. Of the seven years he owed to James, he had only two more to go. Then he would be free as air.

"Where will you live?" I asked. "Will you stay in New Plymouth?"

"Not at all. I'll be off to Naumkeag or Boston as fast as I can. That's where the big money will be, you'll see. I'll be a trader in food. People must eat every day. Soon there will be so many that they will not all be able to grow their own food. They will have to pay for it, even when the bad times come. Do you know, if I had a whole field of onions now, I could double my profit in a few weeks. The only trouble is that I have no land to start with."

He was prepared to work for another seven years if necessary, saving every penny, piling up the money that would then be all his own. But first he would learn to read and write and figure, as the children were learning to do in our school. Without that, he said, he would never rise in the world.

"Two years from now, you'll see me sitting there with my slate," he said, "and you'll never have a more willing pupil."

Two years from now! I could feel a dryness around my heart at the thought of it. What could I say but, "Of course, Adam. You will learn as well as anyone else."

As Christmas came closer, Rebecca and I began to think of the good times we always had at home then. Granny Meg and my mother would begin their preparations months in advance, with a plum cake made of fruit they had dried and stored in September. They would make great plans for the things that would go into it, including spices and rum and butter and white flour and sugar. There would be a plum pudding as well, made with suet, boiled in a cloth for what seemed an eternity, filling the house with sweetness.

For the whole week before Christmas, the wassail bowl was always carried from house to house, and we sang carols and hymns and drank a little of it. Then, on Christmas Day, after church we would spend the day at games and visiting and feasting.

In New Plymouth no one spoke of Christmas at all. We listened eagerly, but not a word was said. James always began the day with prayers of his own composition, but even on Christmas Day itself, there was no mention of it. We knew not what to do. We had never before failed to make this a day of rejoicing and play and happiness.

The two servants joined in the prayers, as usual, but they complained when James sent them to work at their chores immediately afterward. Adam said, "How about a holiday, being as how it's Christmas?"

"Christmas," said James, "is one of the rags of Rome, Popish, anti-Christian. Who knows when Christ was born?"

Paul never had a word to say in his own defense, but Adam was always able to speak for himself. He said, "Since we don't know, surely we can pick on a day for it. I'm a churchgoing Christian, as you can't deny. It goes against my conscience to work on Christmas Day."

This was a shrewd attack. Being only a servant, Adam had no rights, but James was forever talking about conscience and how it must lead us all to godliness. He was not to be bested, however. He said, "In the beginning we had trouble with some of the Strangers who wanted to make merry on Christmas, as they called it. They would not work but went to play openly in the street, at pitching the bar, and stool-ball, and other sports. Governor came to them and took away their implements, and a law was made that such as will not work on that day must keep to their houses. Open reveling in the streets was never allowed again. So if you will not work, you may spend the day in the cowshed at your prayers."

Adam chose to go to work. I was in great fear while this conversation was going on lest James might ask how the servants knew it was Christmas. Rebecca and I had told them when they asked about it. They knew very well that they would not be allowed to celebrate it, but perhaps because of our presence, Adam plucked up his courage at least to ask.

Moses knew the date, too, but he would not have dared to speak of it. Aunt Abigail constantly warned him against expressing any criticism of the way the Saints conducted the affairs of the town, though naturally she kept this advice for times when the Clarks were absent.

Soon after Christmas, I picked up a fever that would not leave me. I was sitting at home trying to cure it, in a chair at the other side of the fire from Moses. It was early afternoon, already getting dark, a cold, wet wind howling around the house. Dinah was out with the chickens, which seemed to have a disease, too. Rebecca was carding wool, and it lay in a great soft heap around her feet. I was happy to be at home where I could watch her.

Aunt Abigail was boiling up some concoction at the fire. As she knelt on the hearth to stir her pot, the blazing logs sent a glow into her cheeks that suddenly made her look like a young girl. I thought I had never in all my life seen her look so contented and happy.

Moses, on the contrary, was looking very glum. He was watching her, too, moving restlessly in his chair. Suddenly he said, "We would have a good enough life of it here, if we didn't have those Saints to contend with day and night."

Aunt Abigail turned in alarm to stare at him, holding her spoon high in her hand. "Brother Moses," she said, "unless you want to go back to the wilderness, you must keep a shut mouth. Beggars can't be choosers. You have had your fling and a dear one it was to you. Now count your blessings."

"Indeed, I do, sister," said Moses. "But James and his preaching get on my nerves. I think I might be a Saint myself, if he didn't shove it down my throat as he does."

Aunt Abigail said, "To give him his due, he never questions you about your time out with the Prices."

"That is true."

None of us had questioned him either, being perhaps afraid of what we might hear. Now, to our surprise, he began to tell us about it. The warm room, the companionship of his old friends and the fact that we were all alone may have moved him to begin, and until Dinah came back, he kept adding more and more to his story, talking very slowly and softly, almost as if to himself, "They took me in, the Prices. No questions asked. I landed on their doorstep and they let me join with them in everything they did. I thought it a fine life, with no one to care for but ourselves, off hunting as long as we liked, home to sleep or not as the fancy took us. The woods are marvelous by night in the height of summer. There are little clearings where we could see the stars and make a shelter of branches and rest there until morning. The dogs kept off wolves and bears. I was never afraid there, not even that the Indians might come.

"We went to the traps every day, and I thought them great experts. They always seemed to get the best animals, and we would skin them and take the pelts home and hang them to dry, and they would talk about when they would be rich and never have to go hunting again. Now and then we came into town to the tavern, and they paid for all and never asked me to put in anything. Why should they? I was working as hard as any of them, and I thought I was due whatever was spent on me.

"Then the host refused to let us into the tavern here in Plymouth and we had to forage farther, I know not where. Sometimes we'd bring home a keg to have in the house by ourselves. That was how I found out what they were at. I was a fool not to have seen it before.

"They got very drunk one night and they began to talk and laugh and joke about the way they were collecting a tithe of pelts from all the traps and never doing any trapping themselves. They said no one could call it stealing, because the creatures didn't belong to anyone in particular. It was every man for himself.

"I've known some thieves but never any who stole from their own kind. Winter was coming on, and they began to put their catch together. It wasn't worth much, because we were always too drunk to take proper care of it. When they tried to sell it, the men who had been robbed were waiting for them. They beat them senseless and took what they could from them.

"I was lucky to get away. I slipped off into the woods and lived for a while in one after another of the shacks we had built. The Indians were good to me. They gave me food whenever I went to them for it. In their own way their huts were cleaner than the house that the Prices had. If any of you had seen that, you would be shaken out of your lives."

I kept quiet. Moses looked and spoke so sadly that I would not for the world have told him that I had seen the lair he had lived in. After a pause he went on, "So at last, when I was near to death from the cold, I decided to come home, knowing I would get a good welcome and care to keep me alive. God knows why I should live at all now, after the things that I have done."

Rebecca said, "It's good to see you sitting there, Father. You can forget all that now. None of us knows anything about this country yet. It will take a good while to learn."

We were all silent for a long time. Then Aunt Abigail said, "I think we should go about building a house of our own. The Clarks are good to us, but we can't live with them forever."

"What would we live on?" Moses asked. "With my feet useless, I won't be much good at farming from now on, I think."

"Everyone that comes to ask my advice brings a little present," Aunt Abigail said. "It may be a bag of beans or a bushel of wheat or some onions or a fish, but it's enough to show that we would never starve. Edward and Rebecca have taught me to read, and I have all the knowledge of the book to help me. We must put our trust in God and make our own way."

My head was spinning with the fever but I was just able to say, "It's good advice, Goodman Moore. We must all follow Aunt Abigail now."

Then, as if the effort of making that speech was too much, I fell off my chair in a dead faint.

Nine

I LAY FOR A WEEK between life and death, barely knowing what was happening around me. Aunt Abigail nursed me, making me swallow her favorite remedies, until she had so many other patients that I had to take care of myself. It seemed that half of the people of New Plymouth were struck down with the same fever. So many were dying that the new governor, Master Winslow, ordered a special day of prayer and humiliation, to ask God's mercy.

They had reason to be afraid, knowing as they did that the Indians who had farmed the same land had all died in one winter. Lying in my bed, I had time to consider whether the reason there were so few living in this Land of Promise might be that it was not made for man to live in at all. The Saints had survived because they were hardy roots. It was no place for the delicate, of mind or body.

Aunt Abigail was the kind of stock that was needed.

It never seemed to occur to her that she might catch the fever herself.

"If you live to be fifty, you'll live forever," she said when I suggested this to her. "I often heard my grandmother say that."

"And are you fifty?"

"How should I know? You haven't taught me to cipher yet."

I found the part of the book where there was information about winter fevers and read it to her until she was word perfect. Instead of giving the sick people only milk, she went back to her old cure — beer, with bread. They were to have eggs, poached or boiled, at least one every day. There were wild duck in plenty, and she prescribed these boiled, with all the fat taken off, even from the soup. They were to be eaten with turnips or a potato.

No one had ever heard of such ways of treating fever, but the rate of recovery proved that she was right. Those who stayed with the old way of starving out the fever fared far worse.

She trained her patients to do exactly as they were told and would stand no argument from them. Even when they felt well again, they dared not step outside the door until she gave them leave, and then only for a short time.

I was no sooner able to move about than Rebecca was taken ill. Kate had got the fever, and Rebecca wouldn't hear of anyone else nursing her. She went every day to the Prences' house, where Kate was living, and spent all day with her, sometimes even sleeping the night, until she was getting better. Then, as Kate began to recover, Rebecca was stricken.

It was agony to see her lie there so still, with all her lovely hair on the pillow, her eyes glazed with the fever so that she scarcely knew me when I was with her. I would sit holding her hand by the hour, hoping to feel some change in her, promising God all kinds of impossible things if only she were to get well.

I went for a whole day to church, never more willingly in all my life, and heard with horror how many had died, old and young. Pastor Smith spoke kindly to us, saying that we must not think this was a scourge of God for our sins, that a loving God allows evil to strike us so that we will come to our senses and not long too much for the things of this world, and to give us a chance to show our love and care for each other. Then Chief Elder Brewster stood up and said, "There is one woman who has shown that love a thousandfold, a Stranger among us only a few months ago, now a very Saint. There she is."

He pointed to Aunt Abigail, who was sitting among the women as quiet as a mouse. All the heads turned to stare at her, until she blushed with embarrassment. Master Brewster went on, "As the Book of Proverbs says: 'Who can find a virtuous woman? For her price is far above rubies. She stretcheth out her hand to the poor, yea, she reacheth forth her hands to the needy. She openeth her mouth with wisdom, and in her tongue is

112

the law of kindness.' Blessed are we here in New Plymouth to have such a virtuous woman among us!"

You may be sure that after such a testimonial, no one disagreed again with Aunt Abigail's methods.

Whether through the prayers of Pastor Smith and Teacher Williams, or through the passage of time, at last the sickness was gone. Certain it is that from the day I spent in church, Rebecca began to get better, though she had a weakness in her breathing for a long time afterward. No more than Aunt Abigail, neither James nor Dinah got the fever, though it almost carried away William. We were luckier than most households — scarcely one of them escaped without at least one death.

The long, gray days continued, with sometimes a burst of sunshine to prove to us that the spring would come someday. When William and I were able to work again, we went on building his house, and I continued to teach in the school with Rebecca. No cultivation was possible, with the cold and the rain and the storms that came roaring in from the Atlantic every few weeks.

Like Moses, I found that it grew harder every day to listen to James Clark, droning out his sermons at all hours of the day and night. When he began, we of Beacon would go silent and wait for peace to come again. Most of his talk seemed to be directed against Aunt Abigail, though she did everything possible to please him. He could not tolerate the fact that she was so wise, though only a woman, and had received public thanks in the church. Then, to make things even worse, Dinah asked Rebecca to teach her to read.

"I could never go to the school," she said. "James wouldn't allow it. But you could teach me a little at home. I could be thinking of it when I'm going around the house, doing my jobs, and when I go out to the hens. Sister Abigail says it's not so hard. It never even gave her a headache, she said, though James says it will do that to me."

"Have you asked him, then?"

"Only once. He got so angry with me, I couldn't ask him again. God help him, I think he wants to have something that I can't have, though surely he has plenty already. But you could teach me when he's out, and he would never know."

It seemed a reasonable thing to do. Rebecca showed her the letters, and Dinah made a good start. She was always afraid that James would find out, and she kept her slate well hidden when he was at home.

James must have suspected something, but without proof he couldn't say a word. He took to opening cupboards and searching in them, taking things down from shelves and looking behind them, then gazing at poor Dinah in a meaningful way. He never said what he was looking for, but he developed a habit of wrapping his Bible in a cloth and putting it away in the chest where he kept his papers, as if he feared that one of us would take it out and read it privately in his absence.

At last William's house was finished, the roof on and

the shutters in place. We gave him some of our paper, which we glazed with linseed oil, so that it was not too dark inside the house. Some day he would have glass, he said, but that would have to wait. It was a good house, higher up the hill than his father's, so that he could look down toward the ocean and be the first to see the ships coming.

"Now we'll get to building yours," he said.

"Not yet," I said. "I must wait a little longer."

William said, "As you please. When you want to begin, I'll be here."

I could not tell him my thoughts, since he had been so good to me always. I had made up my mind to quit New England and go back to Beacon at the first opportunity, but his whole future lay in this wild place and he must battle with it for the rest of his life. He had no choice, whereas I had, and so had Rebecca. It seemed to me that it would be an unmannerly thing to tell him my decision, though some day soon it would have to come out.

Andrew's return made everything easier. As long as I live, I'll never forget the evening he and the two Cutlers walked into the kitchen. Andrew said, "Everyone here?"

Kate was with us, working at the spinning with Rebecca, going over the carded wool to make sure that there were no briars stuck in it. Moses was whittling a piece of wood for the rail of a broken chair. Aunt Abigail and I were sitting at the table with *The Practice of Medicine*. She was tracing the lines with the forefinger of her right hand, as she went along. James was mending a spade. He had at last bought an ox to plough with, but there would still be plenty of digging to do, as he reminded us.

Dinah was making a quilted cap for James, which he said was nonsense, but every now and then he would sneak a look to see how she was doing. Master Bradford had several handsome ones that he wore for special occasions, and also a fine pair of green drawers. Dinah was planning something of the kind for James, too.

Since he was one of the few men who could read, James could never see why he was passed over in the councils of the town. The reason was that he bored everyone to distraction, but more than once he had suggested to Dinah that it was because she didn't make him good enough clothes.

We all leaped to our feet when the three hunters marched into the room. They were looking as healthy and well as ever I saw men look.

"We went to the Prences and heard you were all here," Andrew said.

Rebecca ran and hugged him. Kate was hugging Stephen and Jack, with an arm around each. Then Andrew took possession of her, holding her close for a long moment.

Dinah made everyone sit at the table and put a plate of fresh cornmeal buns in front of them. James got out the strong waters and began to make a punch, going at it solemnly as if it were a difficult chore, but he stopped continually to listen to them as they talked.

They had had a glorious time. Andrew's eyes sparkled with excitement as he told us about the forests they had penetrated, the huge lakes with a cover of solid ice, so that you could glide across on snowshoes, the rivers where beavers built their dams by felling trees, the snowy mountains where the lions and bears lived, the deer and moose.

The Cutlers knew a great many of the Indians and could move from one settlement to another, finding shelter as they needed it and trading for the pelts that would be brought to them at Plymouth during the next few months. The Indians would do the work of scraping and drying and softening them, so that they could be baled at once, ready for *The Swallow*'s first visit.

"I wish we could take the pelts with us," Jack said. "If we pay for them, we never see them. If we don't pay, there's always the danger that the French will come with trading goods and take the furs that were promised to us. We've made up our minds to go back and set up a trading post, where we can store our own goods and trade for theirs. It's the only way to do it."

"Where will you go?" James asked.

"North," said Stephen. "We can't trade with the Abnaki on the Kennebec, which is where we would like to go. Master Brewster and his partners have a tight hold of that. But there are other places, and we will be welcome."

"And I'll be in with them," Andrew said. "Edward, I'm longing to show you the places I've seen."

"When we find a good place, on a broad river, we'll

need all the help we can get," Stephen said. "We must build a strong wooden house that will keep out the cold, and a store as well. We'll need a pinnace or at least a shallop, to get us to the ships when they come."

"Edward built a boat during the winter," Kate said. She was sitting close by Andrew, clearly as excited about the plan as he was. "You'll need to stock up with things the Indians want, even before *The Swallow* comes. Mistress Prence is very good to me. She might persuade her husband to sell us some of their stock, they have so much."

In spite of myself I was getting interested in their talk. Andrew had found what he wanted — the animals and the huge rivers and mountains that made Beacon seem so small and far away. It began to seem a cowardly thing not to join them, not to throw in what skills I had and help to make their enterprise a success. I knew very well what a huge undertaking it was, fit only for hearty, strong men like us, and it was true, as Stephen said, that they would need every pair of hands they could get.

Anyone could see that Kate had already decided to be one of the party. I began to watch Rebecca, trying to see into her mind. Soon I perceived that she was watching me, too. It looked as if each of us was planning to abide by the decision of the other.

James handed around the punch and we all drank some. It was only when he took the bowl to Moses that the visitors noticed his crutches and that he couldn't

118

come to the table. He had been very quiet, though interested in what they were telling us. Seeing Andrew's shocked look he said, "Frostbite. I was foolish."

"We've been chattering so much, we haven't asked for your news," Andrew said. "Thomas Prence said there was a fever but that you are all well now."

"We are well of the fever. We didn't all get it," Dinah said, "though it struck almost every family. Did they tell you about sister Abigail, how she doctored everyone, and was praised for it before the whole body in the Common House?"

They hadn't heard this news, nor that William's house was finished, nor that we had opened the school, nor that Aunt Abigail had learned to read. Andrew said in wonder, "So many things, in such a short time."

"That's how it always is," Jack Cutler said. "We go off to the wilderness and cover miles and miles and see marvels of every kind, and at home they get on with the business of living."

The Cutlers stayed with us until bedtime and promised to come early next day to talk about their plans.

I was afraid I would have a hard time of it getting Andrew alone to tell him that none of us wanted to stay any longer with the Clarks. It turned out not to be necessary. We were all waiting eagerly for Stephen and Jack to come in next morning. When they were sitting around the big table, the first thing Andrew said was, "So, let's go over the most important things. We must build two houses, one here in New Plymouth and one as our trading post. The sooner we make a start on the nearer one, the better. Have you spoken to Master Prence?"

"First thing," Stephen said. "He'll get us that two acres that was set aside for him, down near the ocean, and he'll speak to Master Brewster about our venture in the north. So long as we don't use the Kennebec River, he thinks there will be no ill feeling, but he said we should walk cautiously in the beginning."

"Good advice," said James. "Master Brewster is a powerful man."

With the most dangerous part settled, they revealed the rest of their ideas. While they were away on their winter expeditions, they would need someone to mind the store and keep the house in New Plymouth. Andrew said that if Aunt Abigail would find it in her heart to do them this favor, they would be in her debt forever. She and Moses together would be able to manage things between them, especially now that Aunt Abigail was able to read and write.

"Who told you I can write?" she demanded. "I have no skill in that."

"Edward will teach you," Andrew said calmly. "It won't take you long. Well, what do you say?"

"I'm a useless old fool," Moses said. "Why should you want me?"

"You have experience of the Indians and the woods, I've heard," said Jack with a straight face. "You'll know all the dangers and pitfalls."

Of course they had heard of Moses's adventures from the Prences.

"We'll be glad to do it," Aunt Abigail said, "but what about Kate and Rebecca? Are you going to take them off to the woods with you, chasing beaver and deer?"

"Until we get married," Andrew said. "Then they'll have to stay at home, here in Plymouth. The traveling won't be so hard on our next trip. Captain Mullins has promised to bring us out some horses —"

"Horses!" James was amazed. "Even Master Bradford only has one."

"He'll have plenty when ours come," said Andrew. "We'll breed them for everyone, if the captain can get them to us safely. Horses haven't much courage — I'm just afraid that if there's a bad storm on the way, they'll lose their nerve and want to die."

"You talk about them as if they were people," James said. "They're only brute beasts."

"Not horses," Andrew said. "I know."

I had never thought to see James put down so firmly. He didn't like it in the least. He made no direct answer, but his next question was asked in that tight voice that all of us knew so well, "And when do you think you'll have this house of yours ready?"

"All the sooner if we begin at once," Andrew said cheerfully.

And Stephen said, "Master Prence has seasoned oak that he's ready to sell us. No time like the present."

It was good to have Andrew back. But for him, as I

knew well, I would never have succeeded in following Rebecca as I had done, though I should certainly have tried. There was something about the way he did things that made it certain they would come out right.

Sure enough, within a few days we were all busy digging the foundations for the house and the adjoining store. The work went fast because the land had already been cleared of scrub. It was sheltered from the west wind by a little hill, so that its closeness to the bay was not a disaster. They all felt it was worth a great deal to be so near the shore, though some of the men who came to watch warned them of hurricanes and tidal waves that they had seen in the last few years. They admitted, however, that this spot had never been touched by those freaks of nature.

Then, one dark afternoon as we were walking up the hill on our way home, I held Andrew back from the others and said, "When the ships come in the spring, Rebecca and I will go home."

He was silent for a moment, then said quietly, "I had guessed it. I remember that you never wanted to come in the first place. You did it for Rebecca only. What does she say now?"

"For a while she was uncertain, thinking she would have to stay and take care of her father, but now, as you see, Aunt Abigail is well able to do it."

"That's the most astonishing thing I've seen in the New World," Andrew said. "I wish I could have watched her at work."

"You will. She has a trade now, and she's paid for it. You'll see that she enjoys life now as she never did before."

"Does she know what you're planning?"

"Not yet. But we must tell her very soon."

Ten

AT THE VERY END OF MARCH, it seemed that winter might be coming to an end. The dawn was earlier, and the evenings lengthened a little. The ocean was no longer frozen and Town Brook was running freely again. A few finches appeared one morning, and Dinah said, "That's the first sign of spring every year."

She began to turn out chests and cupboards and to brush the soot down from the rafters. James went often to his field to look for signs of growth, though it seemed to me that there was no life anywhere, nor would be for a long time. William and Jane were to be married soon, and they spent as much time as they could at their new house, making tables and chairs and a big bed.

I came home early from the building one afternoon and found Aunt Abigail and Rebecca alone in the house. Even Moses had hobbled outside for a breath of fresh air. There was no time to lose. I took Rebecca's hand and said, "There's something we want to tell you, Aunt Abigail."

"I doubt if you could tell me much that would be news," she said, thinking I suppose that we were going to name our wedding day.

"It's that we must go home when *The Swallow* comes."

She went to stand by the fire, then sat down suddenly in the rocking chair that only Moses used now. After a pause in which we watched her anxiously, she gave a short sigh and said, "You're doing right. For a long time now, almost every night I see your father and mother, and Granny Meg, too, in my dreams. They don't speak, but I know they're asking me to send you home. Don't worry — I haven't told anyone about it. I know what the good people of Plymouth would say — that I'm a witch. I don't know whether your parents are sending me those messages or whether it's my own thoughts that are crowding in on me when it's dark and quiet in the night. Since both of you had the fever so badly I've been thinking this is no place for you."

Rebecca asked gently, "What about you and Father?"

"We'll stay and take care of Kate and Andrew. They're going to need a father and mother if all their high plans are to work out. And I doubt if brother Moses would be willing to go on the deck of a ship again in this life. Besides, what would become of my patients?"

"You would have plenty of patients in Beacon," I said. "You have so much knowledge now, everyone would come to you for help."

125

Aunt Abigail snorted.

"They would not. I know them. They'd say: 'There's Abigail Moore, that married Tom Hunt from over Ryton way, setting herself up to be something she's not, just because she went off to New England for a while. She couldn't keep her own husband alive and now she thinks she can try her hand on ours.' I know them. And it's true that people won't take advice from a person they know well. My Tom just lay down and died, wouldn't pay any heed to me or what I told him. All he would say was: 'What could you know about it?' "

"But you have so much experience now that you didn't have before," I said.

"That would only make it worse. On *The Swallow* no one knew me from a crow, and besides they were desperate. They would have listened to anyone. Little by little I got my courage up to tell them what to do, and now they have faith in me, for good or ill. That's half the battle. The other half is for me to have faith in myself. I've learned more than reading and writing in the few months I've been out here in New England. For you it's different. You don't need to go away from whispering neighbors and ill-natured people — " She stopped suddenly, then said, "No, that's not it, either. There are good and bad people everywhere. We all get tired of looking at the same faces. The Beacon people were tired of looking at mine."

After a moment I said, "Whatever about that, I think this is your place."

"There's just one thing I must ask you," she said. "Must you take away the book when you go?"

The look of anxiety on her face at the thought of losing it would have decided me if I hadn't already thought of leaving it to her. I said, "It's your book now, not mine. I never made any use of it, so I don't deserve to keep it."

"Thank God," she said. "If I lost my book, I'd very soon lose my patients, too. They believe all wisdom is in there, but half the time I'm only pretending to be reading it. There's a strange idea I have — you'll think I'm crazy."

"What is it?"

"I'd like to write down my own cures, so that when I'm dead and gone they won't be lost. Deacon Fuller says he'll help me, and he'll tell me any that he has, that I mightn't know about."

Rebecca asked anxiously, "Aunt Abigail, what will Father say when he hears we want to go back to England?"

None of us could imagine that. In the end, I undertook to break the news to him. When he came in a few minutes later, Rebecca and Abigail went out and left us together. I hardly knew where to begin. I helped him into the rocking chair and then, while I was still standing behind him, I said, "Goodman Moore, we have just been telling Aunt Abigail that we'll go back to Beacon when the ships come out. She wants to stay here, but if you come with us, we'll always take good care of you when we have our own place in Beacon."

"You're a good lad," Moses said, "but hog, dog, nor divil wouldn't get me to cross the sea again. I'm here where God put me, and here I'll stay for the rest of my life."

So Aunt Abigail had guessed right. Besides, Moses had begun a new life so gradually that the rest of us had hardly noticed it. Perhaps because we had decided to leave, from that day onward I found that I saw everything more clearly and noticed things that would once have passed me by.

We would never have expected that Moses would fill the role he did. In that settlement, or town as they called it now, no one ever had a moment to spare or a word to throw away. Except on the Sabbath, everyone was on the go from morning till night, planning, fixing, arranging, working harder than any slave could be compelled to do, to fill their hungry bellies and their insatiable needs.

The misfortunes of their early years had left a mark on them, even on the Saints. It was true that they had come to the New Canaan in the hope of finding freedom to express their religious convictions in their own way, without interference from king or bishop.

But there was another side to the story. The adventurers, who had paid for them to come, drove them without mercy to get a return on their investment, and though they were mostly working for themselves now, they still had the famine fear on them. They could never have enough. Every time they seemed to be doing better, someone or something snatched it away from them again, or so it seemed. There was no time for chat and talk, no time for people to exchange thoughts or comfort each other as they would have done at home in England.

In the midst of this, there sat Moses in his rocking chair by the fire, a sharp knife in his hand and a piece of wood from which he was carving something. It could be a handle for a hoe, or a spindle for a chair, or a doll for one of the Clarks' granddaughters. He kept his eyes fixed on his work, barely glancing up to see who came into the kitchen.

Come they did, one at a time, slipping in quietly and pulling up a stool near him, to tell him their troubles and ask his advice. They were all ages, men and women, sometimes looking for Aunt Abigail to consult her about sickness but more often clients of Moses's own.

Family quarrels were his specialty, daughters-in-law who refused advice about how to run their houses, lazy husbands and sulky wives, sons who were turning to crime and had to be brought back to the ways of righteousness before it was too late — all the details were poured into Moses's ear while he worked his little knife peacefully and listened.

Then, like Aunt Abigail, he would either come up with the remedy at once, or else he would say, "Give me a day or two to think it over. There is hope, but we must be sure to do the right thing. We must pray for guidance and help from God. Above all, you must not tell anyone what we're doing. You must be silent, and pray."

That was the whole secret of his treatment, as he told me when I asked him about it.

"Anyone who learns to be silent will never again have a family fight," he said with a sly smile. "What I teach them is to keep a shut mouth and catch no flies, but I don't put it like that. It takes two to make a fight. When they're used to the idea of silence, I let them say a word or two, not much — just the soft answer that turneth away wrath. It doesn't always work, but most of the time it does."

I asked, "How long does it take? I noticed you often have the same people come back every week."

"It's slow," he said, "but they put up with it because they're starved for someone to listen to their troubles. If I can teach them to count their blessings and be content with their lot, I feel it's worth all the time I spend on them."

"What if they have no blessings to count? Some people's lives are full of pain and sorrow."

"Everyone has something, and they add to what they have every time they thank God for it."

"They hear that same thing in the Common House every Sunday," I said. "Why don't they listen to Pastor Smith?"

"They do listen, but they must hear it from someone that has no axe to grind for himself. At least I think that's the reason they come to me. And I'll tell you a funny thing, boy. The first few times I was preaching contentment, at the back of my mind I was saying to myself: 'Well, Moses Moore, you're a fine one to be talking like this, after all you've done — skipping across the ocean, dragging your unfortunate womenfolk along with you, then living out in the woods with thieves.' But after a while I found that I was taking in all that wisdom myself and learning my own lessons."

"The same has happened to me and Becky in the school," I said. "When we started it, we were barely able to read and write ourselves, and gradually we're turning into scholars."

"I'll tell you another thing," Moses said. "I always loved a good story, going out around the place, hearing what everyone was up to. Now that I can't go out, if I didn't have the company coming to me, after a few years I wouldn't know one of my neighbors from another. Even I have my blessings."

I saw that we had all learned Moses's lesson, though he was the last person in the world I would have thought could teach me anything.

Poor James Clark was hard put to it to keep his patience with that good brother and sister that he had adopted into his house. There was no more rest for him. Even his rocking chair was gone. He was driven to the limit of his endurance, but he held back manfully, only asking me every other day, "How is the building getting on? How soon do you think the new house will be ready?"

And he would look at me like a lost dog that hopes it will be taken inside and given a bite to eat. At last I was able to tell him, "Andrew says we can move to the new house in two days' time."

James flew into action. He almost ran down to look at the house, to make sure it was really true. Then he began to help us to gather our things together so that there would be no delay. He was there when the Cutlers brought the tables and chairs that the carpenter had made, and his was the most willing shoulder under the chests and beds as they were moved in.

When the great day come, first thing in the morning he said to Dinah, "Wife, we must have a feast this evening to celebrate the new house. A turkey roasted, and some ham, and all the family must come." He eyed the rocking chair, then said sadly, "Brother Moses, I'd like to make you a present of that chair. It's more yours than mine now, and I'd like to think of you sitting in it in your new home."

But Moses would not accept it. He said, "Andrew tells me he has one waiting for me. This one must come back to you with my thanks for all the time I've spent in it."

We had the feast, celebrating the start of a new life for some and the return to an old one for others. We slept that night in the new house. All night long I heard the waves roll up onto the shore, and I thrust down the fear that was beginning to oppress me at the thought of the long voyage home.

The weather changed in late April, and suddenly it was summer. I wish I could have brought away a good memory of New England and of the friends I had made there, but it was not to be. We had barely time to begin enjoying the warm weather when a strange fever swept through the town. Now indeed Aunt Abigail needed her book, and if anyone had had a lingering doubt about her skills, that summer would have finished it. The whole town seemed to look toward her to save them, but it was an impossible task.

The children were the first to be struck down. Their parents picked up the disease soon afterward. All three of the church deacons died, including Aunt Abigail's friend and supporter, Deacon Fuller. They had worked day and night together. With his last breath he gave her his books, praying that she would live long enough to hand on whatever knowledge they contained, to be used by her successors.

Both of Chief Elder Brewster's daughters died, Patience Prence, with whom the Cutlers had lived so happily, and her sister, Fear Allerton. Orphaned children were everywhere. We had so many funerals, we could no longer weep.

Now everyone started complaining, demanding to be given land to live on by themselves and loth to receive any more orders from the Saints. Governor Winslow pleaded and threatened, pointing out the danger of provoking the anger of the Lord against the whole colony, but it seemed to be in vain. In the midst of his sorrow, Master Brewster joined with Roger Williams in appealing to the people to take heart and trust in God and so gathered them together in some sort of way. Those who were in reasonable health began to get ready for the coming of the ships.

Rebecca and I had agreed to return on *The Swallow* as we had come, so that we could take charge of the goods that Andrew and the Cutlers had ready to dispatch to England. She was not the first of the ships that year, but we thought it worthwhile waiting for honest Captain Mullins.

One afternoon at sunset, there came *The Swallow* sailing around the point we called Gurnet's Nose, heading for New Plymouth. Now suddenly we knew what was happening to us: though we loved England and our home there, we had bonds of love here too, which looked as if they would be cut forever.

We had plenty of time to become accustomed to the idea. *The Swallow* had a big cargo, which had to be unloaded and stored and our goods taken on instead. The flour and sugar that had come were very welcome after the harsh diet that everyone endured at winter's end. There were rolls of cloth to guard against next winter's cold, tools and guns and gunpowder, without which no hunting could be done, and for defense — there were no luxuries, nor space for them on the ship.

Timothy Johnson, who had after all made one more voyage, looked for me immediately he came ashore, saying, "Alive and well, thank God. Every year when I come back, some of my friends are missing. How is your girl? Is there fever?"

"Raging, but none of us have got it so far. We had it in winter."

"I have a letter for you, from your father."

"I'll see him soon. We're going home."

"Not many do, but I'm glad of it. And the others? The old brother and sister, and the young man, Hogdon?"

"All staying on. We're the weaklings."

Though they tried to conceal it, this was the general view of our departure. Several people spoke to us and asked us not to go. Then Master Bradford sent for us a few days before *The Swallow* sailed, and we sat with him as we had done when he asked us to open the school, when he was governor.

"So you're going away," he said. "You know we need you, both of you. Every strong man who is willing to work is needed, and Rebecca is not only our teacher but an example to all the young women in the town."

I said, "We've asked Mistress Bridget Fuller to take over the school, and she's willing, now that her husband is dead. My parents need us. They're growing old, and they have no daughter at home. We can't be in two places at once. And there is something else."

I hesitated, feeling that what I was about to say was uncivil, but Master Bradford said, "Go on, boy. Speak your mind. There is always virtue in the truth."

"Neither Rebecca nor I chose to come to New England," I said. "That is the real reason why we should go home now, when we can. You and Chief Elder Brewster and Deacon Fuller and the rest — all of you came from choice, to find peace and freedom. Others came to make a better life. It's good for them to stay too. But not for us. Our home is in Beacon, and we have no need to look further."

"There will be trouble in England soon," he said, "but as you feel you're doing right, I can say no more. Perhaps you will come back to us some day."

"Perhaps."

We knew that we would see Andrew and the Cutlers in Beacon from time to time, and we made plans to send them wool from our own sheep as they needed it, for trade. The hardest of all was leaving Moses and Aunt Abigail, though as usual she was very brisk when the moment of our departure came.

"You'll tell Granny Meg about us," she said. "I wish I could be there to hear her laugh when she hears that brother Moses is the sage of New Plymouth. If she doesn't believe you, tell her to come out here for a visit and she can see for herself." She took us by an arm each and held us close. "The world is small, after all. You're young and strong. Perhaps you will come to see me once, before I die."

Though I thought it very unlikely, this time I said, "Yes, we will come."

For all I know, some day we may.